ROSWELL

A Literary Collection

TABLE OF CONTENTS

Leave No Trace

by Misty Urban

Beep.

The rhythmic chirp of the metal detector sounded like a heart monitor, the kind hooked up to critically ill patients. It gave off a steady, contented chime as I skimmed the flat head of the sensor over the coppery red sand clumped with cheat grass and creosote.

"Hey, chica," Nik called, "if you find the next Mojave Nugget, I want a cut."

She lounged in the Jeep in the shade of a mesquite, feet propped on the sidebar, reading a book for class. I paused a moment to admire her long, toned legs and the taut muscle of her arms and shoulders. She'd been working out with her boyfriend in addition to taking twenty credits this semester, and the stress had purified her somehow, bringing her bone-deep beauty into relief. It was rare I could lure her away for one of my prospecting weekends these days.

I wondered if she'd told Paolo about me. Not the whole truth, I'd bet.

A find like the Mojave Nugget would pay for both our master's degree programs, but I wasn't looking for gold. I checked the display of my uncle's old Weekender for remaining battery power. Enough to last till sunset, if Nik held out that long.

"I found a buffalo nickel last weekend," I told her.

She hadn't been with me. I'd also found an old horseshoe, a watch strap, and three more arrowheads. The lost and broken remnants of other lives. But not the life I was looking for.

"Nice," she said without looking up from her book. "Exterminate the native species and the indigenous peoples, and then commemorate them on a coin. The American way."

"Mm-hmm." I swung the detector around a tarbrush. *Beep*. Nik was an enrolled member of the Mescalero Apache Tribe. For five years our weekends had been this: leave Las Cruces Friday after our last classes, squinting into the glare of sun rebounding off White Sands. Stop in Alamagordo for Lotaburgers from Blake's and take them to Nik's mom's for dinner. Leave the reservation before dusk and point the headlights down the long lonely highway toward Roswell, emerging from the lush green of Lincoln National Forest into sandy brown desert scrubland, passing the Rio Hondo and the empty flat reservoir of Two Rivers Dam. We'd be in Border Hill before my mom and Donnie had finished watching the news.

Then Sunday night, or whenever my mom got on my nerves, the reverse: the three-hour drive back to the New Mexico State campus, through rippled desert foothills and mountainous forest, past the missile silo, the Air Force base, the national parks and monuments and refugesand wildernesses, all the U.S. government's attempts to manage and tame and use this magnificent land. Sneaking through the gap in the San Andres as the hindquarters of oryx fled from our headlights, dragging ourselves exhausted and hungry into our apartment in University Park. All those hours in the car together, amounting to weeks if not months, and we never got bored. Never fought. Talked about anything and everything.

Well, almost everything.

The sensor ticked in its steady rhythm as the October sun ticked higher in the sky. *Beep. Beep.* It was a pleasant day, a dry mid 80s, the air shimmering against the foothills of the distant mountains. Beneath a tall yucca I caught the pair of flat, shining onyx eyes before the haregathered itself and sprung away, its ears sweeping the air like wings.

"Black-tailed jackrabbit," I called to Nik, who liked to hear about the wildlife. My heart beat faster at the brief scare, swinging like the needle on the Weekender's display.

"Someone's dinner," she answered. "I saw bobcat scat near the road when we went into Salt Creek to check on the camper." She put her finger in her book and looked at me over it. "That where we're sleeping tonight?"

"If you don't mind. Donnie's a mess right now. It will freak him out to have extra people around, and we'll have to hear him talk endlessly about whatever new shit someone's come up with in the alien conspiracy theory world."

Her eyebrows lifted above the large round frames of her sunglasses. I resisted the urge to ask if she'd put on sunblock. She hated when I tried to mother her.

"Did the UFOlogist Invasion happen this year?" she asked.

"Nope, canceled due to COVID, like everything else. But he's trying to organize a virtual conference, and honestly . . ."

Nik found my older brother's obsession endearing. Donnie worked in the gift shop of the International UFO Museum and Research Center, and while UFO tourism kept my town alive and Donnie's job got me all the space candy I could stomach, there's a point when the little green men jokes start to wear on a girl.

Nik shrugged. "It makes him happy."

"I know. But should it, though?" I was starting to sweat beneath the bandana I'd tied around my head, which doubled as a mask if we needed to go indoors. I was tired of saying this to every person who asked stupid questions when they learned where I was from. "It just never gets through to him that the Roswell incident has been debunked. Come on, the debris from the 1947 crash was an experimental spying device made by Project Mogul. We had Robert

Goddard testing his rockets, the 509ᵗʰ Bomb Wing at the Roswell base. People around here are used to stuff blowing up." I itched at a rolling bead of sweat. "But then these New Age cranks come along in the 1970s with their wild ideas about Area 51, getting people to talk about weird stuff they thought they saw thirty, forty years ago, thinking the bodies from the Air Force dummy drops are alien beings. Then the government says releasing UFO-related information would pose a national security risk, and my brother bites on the conspiracy theories, hook, line, and sinker."

"You don't need to tell me again." Nik turned the page of her book. She was reading Terry Tempest Williams' *Refuge* for her environmental justice class. I pointed at the cover.

"I say to him, you want to talk about government conspiracies, let's talk about White Sands. Talk about the Trinity test. Oppenheimer's Gadget." My throat closed. Talk about the silica in the desert sand fused into trinitite, like a thousand shattered radioactive green soda bottles, new elements created by wrenching apart atoms and smashing them together in wrong ways. Talk about how Fat Boy, tested here and dropped on Nagasaki later, melted 40,000 people into broken green glass in one day. "Then the Nevada Test Site. Then the Marshall Islands." Thousands of clouds of radioactive elements released into the air so the U.S. could be the most feared country on earth.

"Cami. I get it," Nik said gently. "Your government has been trying to kill my people for two hundred years. Why is a shock to anyone that their own people are collateral damage?

Beep. Beep. Beep. The metal detector was going loco, the needle swinging wildly. My arm shook in the cuff. My skin was brown, which wasn't unusual around here. Half of Roswellidentified as Hispanic. Donnie was handsome and tall and blonde, like his father. I had my Mexican father's straight black hair and brown eyes. And Billie, my little sister—I couldn't remember what her father had looked like. I couldn't remember what Billie had looked like, either, not without looking at a picture. It had been so many years.

Beep. Beep.

So many years of searching, finding nothing, not a belt buckle, not a trace—where had she gone? Where could she be? It was the mystery that kept me awake at night, that brought me out of a sound sleep gasping with panic, drowning in my own bed. Nowhere was safe when I didn't know about Billie. *Beep. Beep. Beeeeeeeep.*

"Got something!" Nik yelled, throwing her book aside and vaulting out of the Jeep.

She grabbed a trowel from the tool belt around my waist and we scrabbled together, red desert sand flying. My heart wailed like a siren in my ears. Small. Silver. Like a child's bracelet. A child's silver-

10

linked bracelet, spangled with small metallic triangular things, caked with dirt.

My heart stopped beating. It could be hers. It was possible. Billie had a bracelet she'd worn everywhere.

My fingers curled around the find, trembling. Finally, after all this time, I might know the truth.

I worked while Nik cleaned up our dinner of microwave enchiladas and mixed usmargaritas. We didn't get phone service or internet out here in the wilderness, so she started looking through my uncle's DVD collection. It was heavy on Roswell documentaries, UFO conspiracies, and alien invasion disaster movies.

"Ooh, I haven't seen this in years." Nik popped *Independence Day* into the DVD player and put up her feet. "Watch with me?"

"I'm almost done here. I've just about got the tags clean. It's a charm bracelet or something." My hands still shook as I dipped my tiny brush in the water and patiently, slowly, painted away the red sand caked into the design of the dangling tags and between the silver links of the bracelet. It wasn't Billie's. It looked older than anything of hers would be, and besides, the whole point was to prove there was nothing of Billie's around here. She wasn't here.

11

Nik stretched her arms behind her head. I tried not to stare at the long lines of her body, lean and lithe as a cat. "Character you'd sleep with," she began, a game that had seen us through way too many college drinking parties.

"Jasmine, the exotic dancer and kickass single mom. Duh."

Nik nodded. She could guess my answers already, but asked anyway, just to ask, or to prove how well she knew me. "Marry."

"Hmm. Miguel. He's going to be a fine man in a few years."

This surprised her. "Not Will Smith?"

"Will Smith can be my sloppy seconds if Miguel doesn't work out." I dug with a wooden scraper into the grooves emerging on one of the charms: the initials CFG. My chest squeezed with relief. Nothing to do with Billie.

"Character you'd sleep with," I asked Nik, pretty sure I knew her answers, too.

She held silent for a long moment, then said, "I'm moving to Berkeley with Paolo."

My scraper skidded across the metallic charm and stabbed my palm. I sucked in a breathand put it down on the table. After a long, long moment I raised my eyes to look at her.

"Berkeley?" It might as well be the moon.

She nodded, watching the TV. "He got offered a postdoc at the Berkeley Lab next year. I applied to the Ph.D. program in environmental science."

On screen, something exploded. It covered the painful bang of my heart. "Wow," I managed. "That's—that's really great."

She'd chosen. He'd won.

I picked up my brush, hands shaking. "What did your Mom say?"

She laughed. "She said our kids will only be one-quarter Apache blood, but they can still be registered in the tribe."

"Kids. Whoa." I sucked in air. "I guess I could come visit you. Maybe bring Donnie up to see the SETI Research Center. He'd go nuts."

She glanced over, saw my face, and her feet hit the floor. "Cami. Hey." She walked over to the small dinette table where I sat hunched beneath a work light, my tools scattered over an old newspaper. Try as I might to air this place out, my uncle's camper always smelled like mildew and stale cigarette smoke. It was going to poison me, given enough time.

She reached for my hand, but I clung to my tools, brushing, brushing at the clinging dirt. This coppery bloody red was what made the bluffs of the Salt Creek Wilderness so famous. There was such a unique ecology in this place, where the Chihuahuan Desert met the

13

plains of the Llano Estacado. The Bitter Lake refuge was a waystation for migratory birds and riparian species that made their home along the Pecos. The strange sinkholes, what we called the Bottomless Lakes, had fish found nowhere else. And this was Nik's native land, the homeland of her people. She had been born within the anchor of the four sacred mountains. As her rite of passage she had dressed in her buckskins and for eight days touched no water, drinking through a reed, eating roasted mescal heart, channeling the qualities of White Painted Woman.

The Mescalero had their myths of alien invasion as well. When giant monsters threatened the People, White Painted Woman withdrew to the mountains and gave birth to Killer of Enemies. She reared him in cunning and bravery and when he grew to be a man he slew the monsters and ensured the People would live forever in safety and peace.

How could she leave all this for Berkeley?

"I don't know what this is," I muttered, throwing the bracelet down.

She picked up the silver links in her delicate hands, examining the dangling charms. "It's one of those Wohelo thingees from the Campfire Girls. You know, another one of those social organizations white people founded that encourage them to imitate and appropriate 'Native American' cultures."

My mom had been a Campfire Girl. I knew what Wohelo stood for. She'd make fun of it sometimes, standing on the stained linoleum of the kitchen after another late night at the bars, looking through the cabinet for snacks and feeling sorry for herself. "Work, health, love. That's what the Campfire Girls taught us," she told me a thousand times, when I snuck downstairs in my bare feet and thin rayon nightie to make sure she didn't leave a cigarette burning near the curtains, that she'd turned off the stove. "That's supposed to keep everything in balance. Work, health, love." She said the words like a curse, slamming the door shut on the fridge full of processed cheese and ham slices. "What the hell happened?"

"Cami." Nik's voice came from a long way away. "Hey. Are you mad?"

"No. Of course not. I'm happy for you." That was a lie. My jealousy choked me. "I just—Berkeley. And I'll be stuck here in Roswell, teaching at the New Mexico Military Institute or Eastern New Mexico University, spending my spare time . . ." Doing this. It would never end. I'd never leave Roswell, not until I had answers. Not until we finally knew.

On the movie, the countdown ended, and the dark metallic discs parked over the world's cities opened their evil hulls. The weapon charged. The air hummed. And then the impact, the blazing column of light, the explosion, concentric rings of fire leaping outward, turning

15

everything, cars, people, buildings, futures to ash in seconds. Just like Alamagordo.

Nik put both of her hands in mine. This was a big thing for her. She wasn't affectionateby nature. Her mother had named her after the female assassin on a TV show she loved. Her father, so she'd been told, was a serviceman on Holloman Air Force Base. He was handsome. After he was reassigned to another base and Nik was born, Shanta, Nik's mom, tried to find him. She looked him up in the directory and called the number. A woman answered. Sounds of children, a baby crying in the background. She hung up.

It could have been the TV, we say every time she tells this story. It could have been a neighbor's kids. Sure, she says, but she never tried again.

Nik and I have looked him up and found a number of people he could be: a plumber in Pennsylvania, a school board president in Michigan, a hog farmer in Alabama. We tell stories about him and his second wife, the other children he left scattered at Air Force bases around the world. I've never felt the urge to call my dad, either, though we make up stories about him, too. Our absent fathers, the mythological grounding of our lives.

White Painted Woman gave birth alone, and so did Shanta. My mother tried hard to keep her men around, but they disappeared, one by one.

16

"Cami." Nik held my hands, looked into my eyes. "You ever going to tell me what you're looking for?"

In Roswell, everyone knew. We were that family. We lived with our agony exposed, no cover. When I went away to college it was a relief not to speak of it. I hadn't lied, I just—never told anyone. To say it would make it real, make it happen all over again. Or maybe I was afraid that if I told the story over and over, it might grow into something even more strange and suspicious, like the stories told by the sons and daughters of the ranchers and the army base officers and anyone else who'd touched the debris of the Roswell crash. How they saw it carefully packed and dispatched, some pieces sent to the Wright-Patterson Air Force Base in Dayton, Ohio, where the military analyzed and tried to reverse engineer captured Soviet and German technology, and some pieces to Washington, D.C. And what, Donnie liked to say as if it were proof, what so alarming and otherworldly and wildly dangerous had dropped out of the sky above New Mexico and burned into the ground outside Corona, what was so unusual and important that it got delivered to one of the Air Force's most highly classified operations and the President of the United States?

On screen, a gorgeous and dusty Jasmine wandered with her son and her dog through a landscape of devastation. Beneath our hands, a sixty-year-old bracelet from a lost civilization caught the light.
And finally, I told her.

Told her how Billie's dad came to the house one night and Billie came to the door. I imagined her, seven, bewildered why her dad wanted her now, in her fuzzy pajamas and frizzy braids, asking him if they could take her stuffed rabbit, Boo. He took a whole suitcase, stealing one of Mom's bags while she was checking people out at the grocery store, oranges, hamburger, breakfast cereal, no idea what was hovering overhead. Another alien abduction.

He asked Donnie, playing his video games, if he wanted to come along. Donnie thought about it a minute, said no.

I wasn't there, so I wasn't asked. I was thirteen, misunderstood, hiding somewhere and fuming that I would show them, everyone who hated me, I was going to do something really great and amazing one day—or something really huge and destructive—and then they'd know what I was really capable of, wouldn't they.

What would I have said if he'd asked me?

Every once in a while I dream I was there. Sometimes I yell at him and drag Billie back into the house. Sometimes I take her hand and we hide in a closet, shivering, while he stalks and bangs and yells outside the door. Once I took her hand and we simply floated away, up, up into the air, like balloons.

"But the prospecting," Nik said gently, still holding my hands. Her palms were warm and smooth. She smelled like salt and lime, bitter, delicious.

"We thought, for years, that he'd just taken her somewhere and set up a new life. Maybe changed her name. She was the child on the milk carton, Billie. But then…"

She squeezed my hands, and I choked back sobs. Paolo had won. He was taking her to Berkeley. A place of green and water, so far from here.

"Three years after that—" I paused and gulped. "Remains were found by some hikers on the edge of the Salt Creek Wilderness. A skeleton, some bones. Adult male." Picked clean by the coyotes, bleached by the sun against the copper-red soil, just like in the cartoons. "The dental records matched her father. So did the belt buckle—a big silver triangle with a rattlesnake in the shape of an M."

Nik shivered. "Bad omen animal," she muttered.

"My uncle bought the metal detector and started looking," I said. "After work, weekends, holidays. Soon it was all he did, just to give Mom some peace of mind. I was sixteen, so I started to help him. And then—"

It became an obsession. I started with the maps and grids, tracking the ground he'd covered. Then, after he lost his foot to diabetes, I took over the metal detector, too. I wanted to give my mom the closure she sought. So she didn't circle around endlessly, silenced, never knowing the truth of what had happened here.

Donnie searched in his own ways, scanning the chat groups, the skies. In some ways, I knew, he wanted to believe. Wanted so badly to find another world, perhaps one where he would be normal, not on the spectrum, not a diagnosis, not weird or abnormal or flawed. Where people thought and spoke like him.

Neither of us had been able to find Billie.

"It's that bracelet," I said, wiping my eyes. "She had this charm bracelet she loved. We all bought her things to put on it. They were like talismans to her. I'm sorry, but she would have loved something like the Campfire Girls. She'd have chosen a Zuni name and collected beads and wore fringe at all the stupid ceremonies."

"It's okay," Nik said, still holding my hands. "This isn't hers. If there were no remains, and there's no other trace, then she was never there. She's still out there somewhere. She escaped."

"Do you think so?" I gasped for air. I'd never dared believe that until Nik said it. All my thoughts led to the bones in the wilderness and then stopped. But if Billie wasn't here, then she could be out there somewhere. Alive. Safe. Happy.

I was like the characters on screen, walking into the underground lab and finding the answers laid out before them. Bizarre, unbelievable, almost unfathomable. But the only explanation that made all the fragmented evidence make sense.

Nik sat me on the couch with a margarita and pulled the blanket with Kokopelli over us. We watched Will Smith and Jeff Goldblum clamp cigars between their teeth and fire a nuclear missile into the alien mothership. We watched Randy Quaid drive his plane into the column of light, giving it to the aliens up the ass. We watched brave Americans end the invasion, kill the monsters, save the world. Again.

Much later, as I lay in the dark, listening to the hum of the generators and watching the stars dangle like silver charms, Nik slipped her feet into my bunk, slipped her hands beneath my shirt. I gripped her tightly. She knew me so well.

"Berkeley's so far away, Nik," I whispered.

"It won't end us," she murmured against my hair.

I could tell Paolo. I was sure he didn't know. But what would it achieve?

The truth, I suppose. There are always those who'd rather know the truth.

I held her to me tightly, breathing in lime. Her hair smelled faintly of creosote. She was taking all this to Berkeley to get a Ph.D., and then after that, who knew? I'd choose her every time, the smart, sassy, beautiful woman who'd save her own ass along with a truck full of other people. But I wondered what she'd ever seen in me. Would she ever tell me? Was there anything I could do that would keep her?

Billie would be seventeen now. I imagined her with corkscrew curls, an outrageous natural mop she never tried to tame. I imagined her with the deep velvety eyes and ridiculous lashes of the oryx, the dusty brown skin. That animal had never belonged in New Mexico, either. I imagined her driving a car, planning for college. Smiling as a lover whispered in her ear. I willed her to be out there, alive, on her own sacred mountain. I willed her to have found a world of peace and freedom.

Nik had set me free, too, in a way. Maybe I could finally put away the Weekender and take the trailer somewhere. See Carlsbad, the Gila cliff dwellings, the thousands-year-old petroglyphs. Drive Donnie out to see the Very Large Array—he'd always wanted to go there. All the beautiful mysteries of our planet, right here, laid out beneath those inscrutable, infinite stars.

I understood my brother, sitting night after night in his own SETI setup, listening to his headphones, scanning the sky. He wanted answers. Most of us do.

But holding Nik, biting back all the things I'd never say, I knew I would choose to live with the mystery, the silence. Some things are better left alone. Sometimes, we're better off not knowing the truth.

MARTIAN ARRIVING IN THE MIDFIELD
BY SAM LIGETI

Neon green jersey

And neon green socks —

My infiltration is not exactly subtle.

The chosen girls swirl in graceful waves

Of navy blue and white,

High ponytails bouncing,

Fancy footwork announcing

The barriers to entry for a foreigner like me.

Stepovers and scissors

As easy as walking,

Rainbows and rabonas

Even casually while talking.

Their lean bodies dip and swerve

In time to a beat I can't yet hear.

Aluminum blood seeps into my mouth –

I swallow the taste of fear.

Green girl green skills come to dance with the elite,

An I wanted space invader here to crash their fleet.

During water breaks

Stifled snickers follow me like flies.

I turn around and girls gaze down,

Lingering cruelty twisting their mouths.

Scrutinization is a new sensation and

My hands grip the waistband of my shorts,

which I realize for the first time

Are pulled up way too high.

My hands feel the puff of bangs across my forehead,

Which I realize for the first time

Is their excuse to crucify.

But when my cleats make contact with the grass

And the ball finds its way to my feet,

The whispers grow quiet and the field starts to hum.

A shimmering rectangle of green, my green,

A suspended space

Of clean lines and clear rules

Is where I discover

I can speak their language too.

Break time again and I hope

For a friendly word,

But such optimism's absurd —

First a joke and now a threat,

Louder whispers is what I get.

I realize sucking on ice cubes

And sweating through shin guards

That I have a choice to make for myself.

I stand slowly,

Combatting the sudden weight of gravity.

I brush bits of grass off my knees

And set my sights on the space between two posts.

A week later I find my name written on their roster,

Printed in perfectly legible, lovable letters.

From the rec leagues to the big leagues,

I've been chosen.

Get ready, girls, I think.

A goal scoring green alien

Has landed on your team.

Your fear, you see,

Is not bigger than my galaxy crossing, Universe hopping

Midfield martian

Dream.

Top Secret
By Joseph Stone

December 26ᵗʰ

Walker Air Force Base, Roswell, New Mexico

"Come again, Harris?" Caroe squinted in disbelief.

"The Lieutenant General is sick and won't be coming in," she repeated herself, avoiding the urge to check if her hair was coming loose under her cap. "He just telephoned to have me inform you he'd be out sick the rest of the week. He asked me to confirm for you that his orders still stand."

Caroe stood up from his desk with a start. His light brown eyes wandered around his office aimlessly before he struck the desk with both palms to produce a loud crack of anger. The impact shook the room and knocked his desk calendar clear to the floor, though it remained opened to December 1966.

Major General Dale Caroe was a man of average and unremarkable appearance. His height, build, and face were each plain and perfectly ordinary. Even his light sandy brown hair, which he kept short and neatly cut, appeared just as common as it could. The combination of these attributes hid the explosive volatility of Caroe's personality, and they had deceived many unfortunate souls until it was too late.

"He didn't think that was something he needed to tell me directly?"

JoAnne Harris knew better than to show Caroe the slightest bit of fear. As secretary to Tim Glinatsis, the Lieutenant General in charge of Walker Air Force Base, she knew well enough how Caroe thrived on the intimidation he instilled in the people under his command. JoAnne didn't want to feed the dragon more; this day would already be difficult enough.

"I suggested that same point to him, sir, but he confirmed I should deliver the message to you."

Two days prior, Glinatsis had ordered Caroe to cancel Christmas week vacation for all base personnel handling the transfer of Storage Hangar B. Washington had flagged the base for closure last year because of budget concerns. They scheduled all its equipment for transfer to Edwards Air Force Base in California and Homey Airport in Nevada. The latter base, better known as Area 51, would receive the contents of Storage Hangar B by June of next year when Walker would be finally closed.

Despite the healthy time cushion, the Lieutenant General had ordered the hangar cleared by no later than the end of this year. The enormous undertaking had undergone dozens of setbacks, mostly due to the limits of Doctor Busch's team. As December sped to its conclusion, all involved presumed Glinatsis would grant an extension.

Instead, he ordered that all necessary personnel resume duty, starting the day after Christmas until they completed the job. And none of the twenty-eight men and women impacted were more infuriated than Caroe himself. Now, as the truth washed over him, JoAnne did her best to remain calm as Caroe's blood pressure hit the roof.

"Follow me," he ordered and set off out of his office noisily.

Caroe made for the stairs to the hangar's lower level, moving with heavy clanging footfalls along the steel floors. When he arrived at Doctor Ian Busch's laboratory office, Caroe entered like a raging bull, throwing the door open without the slightest courtesy.

"Report," he ordered sharply.

With a start, the doctor's eyes rose from his paperwork, and he furrowed his brows.

"Good morning, Dale."

"Fuck your good morning, Doctor. You and your bullshit are the reason half our personnel are not at home with their families this morning. Now report before I have Harris go call the closest airman with a side-arm to shoot you in the head."

JoAnne looked down at the ground, attempting not to react.

"Really, this is all my fault? You think I'd rather be here doing this shit instead of being home with my kids? You know good and damn well why here. And if you'd like to help, please keep our boss the hell out of my sight."

"No problem," Caroe broke a sarcastic grin, "Glinatsis is at home with the sniffles. So, I'm the only one you'll need to worry about calling your slow ass to attention."

"You're kidding."

"Nope, he's decided to let us pay our pound of flesh without the courtesy of his presence. But he clearly hasn't motivated you, so perhaps that's for the best."

Doctor Busch attempted to respond, but Caroe held up his hand.

"Now, we can leave here to salvage what remains of our holiday the second after the job is done. So, what's it going to take to finish by the end of today?"

"You're dreaming," Busch shook his head.

"It's all done, but for half of the second floor. What the fuck is taking you so long?"

"Moving airplanes is easier than examining thirty years of classified storage boxes and re-cataloging them. I can't just get inside a cockpit, start the engine up, and fly the whole thing to California. My team is moving through it all as fast as they can."

"Horse shit."

"They are moving as fast as they can, Dale," Busch said, becoming aggravated. "We're talking about five analysts doing the job of twenty. I don't have a fleet of grunts and engineers to get it done like you and Stansfield have. You might as well send your people home until we have more finished containers for them to move."

"Speaking of Stansfield, she's running late because of the snow in Wisconsin. But don't worry, when she gets here, she can also explain why you're a useless piece of shit to keep a mother from her family."

"Have you ever considered changing tactics—perhaps trying to be helpful for once?"

Dale released a burst of healthy laughter at the scientist's sarcasm, and he seemed to relax for the first time since entering the lab.

"Well, I guess anything is possible. All right, let's try it. What could I do to be helpful, Ian?"

"Do you have anyone who can type? I mean seriously type—not just hunt for letters with their index fingers. If I could pair each analyst with a man to do the cataloging, they might move through the contents twice as fast."

"You want knuckle-draggers who know how to type? I'm not optimistic, but I'll go find out right now. What else?"

"I have to do room L2-13 on my own because of the clearance level. Do you or Stansfield know how to type?"

Caroe released another volley of laughter.

"Then it's going to take all week."

"It would thrill JoAnne to assist you," Caroe gestured at her.

"I've thought of that, but she doesn't have clearance for—"

"Horse shit. She's the Lieutenant General's personal secretary. She probably knows more about this place than you and I combined. Now walk her in there and put her to work."

"You're gonna take the heat for that?"

"There's not going to be any heat. No one will give a damn about this when the junk is sitting in Nevada. Just get it done."

JoAnne knew little about Sub-Level Two or its contents. The repository of sensitive materials had nothing to do with the daily operations of Walker Air Force Base or its primary mission. As such, the Lieutenant General had rarely paid attention to the vast subterranean storage hold, referring to it as a hoard of junk, and so neither did JoAnne.

"If this works, we might be finished by tomorrow," Doctor Busch said as he turned the key in the door to L2-13.

"That sounds like a plan," JoAnne answered.

She carried a portable typewriter in her left hand and a ream of cataloging forms in her right arm. She's forgotten their heavy weight since arriving down in the basement. Doctor Busch had led JoAnne through a maze of poorly lit corridors that echoed as if they might go on forever. This floor was more than a little intimidating, and she couldn't help her eyes from moving left and right down every off-shooting path they passed. It was only when they both stopped outside Room L2-13 that she heard the sound of footsteps ringing their approach from behind.

"Doctor Busch?" a voice called out from down the hall.

Advancing under the overhead lamps that hung every twenty feet, it took JoAnne time to recognize the man's face until he was almost upon them.

"Can I help you?" Doctor Busch called out.

"Good morning, Doctor. Master Sergeant Reimer reporting. The Major General assigned me to help you. He believes I have the proper authority to enter this section with you."

"Does he?"

"That's what he just told me, sir," the young man nodded before turning his eyes on Harris to smile. "Hey there, JoAnne."

"Hello, Aaron," she nodded with a smile.

She hadn't realized just how uncomfortable she'd been alone with the doctor down in this basement until her friend joined them.

"Can you type, Sergeant?"

"I can give it a shot, sir."

"He can assist with unpacking and repacking," Harris added on the young man's behalf.

Doctor Busch held the man's gaze for a moment, then turned back to unlock the door.

"Very well," he sighed.

Flicking on the light switch, Ian brought the room to a warm glow, much brighter than the outside hallway.

L2-13 was at least five thousand square feet of space, arranged with hundreds of wooden crates of a dozen different dimensions. They were piled upon one another to form ten rows that rose nearly to the twelve-foot roof. Each container was stamped in black ink with the words TOP SECRET—U.S. Air Force, followed by a unique seven-digit number.

"Our job is to open every single crate and examine the contents against what the original packer noted on our manifest. Once verified, we'll repack the crate, and JoAnne will retype the description onto the fresh forms provided to us."

"There's got to be five hundred crates in here," Reimer said.

"Seven hundred and eight, according to this," Ian held up the hefty file folder, "so this will not be very quick, I'm sorry to say. Still, we've got over eight thousand crates on this level, so be glad that you're not partnered with the teams working outside this room."

"Will I have to type on the floor?" JoAnne asked warily.

"Of course not," Ian answered. "Sergeant, pull out a crate and set it on the trolley there for her. Harris, you'll set your typewriter on top of the crate and roll it down the aisles after us like a shopping cart as we open and repack the boxes."

"That'll work just fine," JoAnne nodded with relief.

Reimer stepped down the short end of the massive room past the makeshift rows to fetch the trolley cart without answering. Turning it around, something caught his eye.

"What happened down there?"

JoAnne and the doctor followed over to where Reimer stood and peered down the last row. Several hundred feet away, it appeared a section of the boxes had collapsed from their stack and littered the ground.

"Damn it," Busch sighed and moved down the row to inspect the damage.

Following with Reimer, JoAnne saw the collapse appeared to be more than an accident. Several smaller crates were shattered along the floor, their contents of rocks and metal parts strewn along the ground for twenty feet or so. It looked as if someone had purposefully thrown them down. A crowbar and mallet lay on the ground beside a box of large nails.

"Did someone already start in this room?" JoAnne asked.

"It looks like someone got into a fight," said Reimer.

"I don't believe so," Busch answered. "But if someone broke in here, we need to survey it at once. JoAnne, go report this to the Major General. He'll want to know."

She turned to leave but paused.

"I don't remember how to get back," she said, not wanting to admit that she didn't want to walk through those dim corridors by herself.

"Left out the door. Then right, left, and left again. At the very end, you'll find the stairs. But if you get lost, don't worry. Just look for the small exit signs—they'll get you there."

Nodding slowly, JoAnne turned and started the trek back alone.

December 27th

After Caroe arrived on the scene and examined the damage, he allowed work to resume without much concern. The manifest descriptions matched what his eyes could see: random unidentified engine parts and rock samples. As there was no evidence of who might have caused the damage, he left them to clean up and resume their work.

By the end of the day, JoAnne had assisted Doctor Busch and Sergeant Reimer to catalog almost one hundred boxes.

Arriving outside the laboratory this morning, JoAnne slowed when she heard two men yelling. The angry voices belonged to Aaron and the doctor.

"…but then I need to go find it in his office. If I have to, I'll take it from the son of a bitch. Help me, damn it. You started this! Don't turn your back on me now!" Reimer shouted. His wild eyes remained locked on the man until noticing JoAnne standing outside the door.

Doctor Busch turned to see her for only a second before lowering his voice to whisper something to the sergeant.

Reluctantly, the younger man left the room in a hurry, avoiding JoAnne's eyes as he passed her.

"I didn't mean to intrude, Doctor," she said when Reimer was gone. "Is everything okay? Are we still on to continue downstairs?"

The doctor didn't answer but kept his back to her.

"Shall I report to the major general instead?"

JoAnne hadn't meant to imply anything by her question, but when the doctor turned to answer, she knew she'd made a mistake.

"It's none of the major general's goddamn business what goes on in my lab," he raised his voice. "But go ahead if it will make you feel better. I need nothing from you."

JoAnne began to answer, meaning to clarify that she had no intention of running to discuss the matter, but the words got caught in her throat. Instead, she turned and left the room.

Technical Sergeant Anissa Stansfield had joined the Air Force in her early twenties. She had faced the expected obstacles ensured by her gender, and the arrival of her son early on had done little to ease them. Still, Stansfield had risen through the ranks well enough so that by forty-three, she was the highest-ranking female officer at Walker Air Force Base.

Stansfield was also the only female officer at the base.

Though JoAnne was not an officer, she often turned to Stansfield to confide sensitive matters. Being secretary to the top man, JoAnne rarely socialized with the other non-officers on the base. The nature of her role often exposed her to information that she must keep secret. Knowing this, most of her contemporaries would often mine her for details that she could never tell them. As a result, JoAnne mostly avoided even causal relationships among the lower ranks. Despite that JoAnne was one of them, it was easier not to talk to those people at all than maintain a vigilent tongue.

But Anissa Stansfield was part of the top circle, and there was little JoAnne needed to keep from the woman. More to the point, JoAnne deeply admired Stansfield and trusted her opinion.

Stepping into her office, JoAnne found Stansfield sitting at her desk, looking sorely exhausted. She gathered her dark blonde hair impatiently back into a bun where the wind had pulled it free.

"Made it out of the snow at last?"

"If I couldn't count on a court-martial, I would've gladly stayed buried in my house. I assume Dale is delighted that I'm a day late."

"Naturally," JoAnne smiled. "It's just been him and Doctor Busch to keep me company. The Lieutenant-General called in sick. He doesn't plan to come in at all until the new year."

Stansfield shot her a furious look of silent disbelief. In time, it melted away to a devious grin.

"Oh, Jesus," she covered her face and laughed. "Dale must be pissed."

"He made a few choice phrases yesterday that I've promised to forget."

"I'm surprised he hasn't shot someone," Stansfield opened her eyes comically.

"He and I discussed shooting the doctor, as a matter of fact," JoAnne nodded her head with a smile.

"Poor bastard."

"The doctor is also upset with me this morning because I walked in on an argument he was having with Sergeant Reimer."

"What about?" Stansfield bent her head slightly with concern.

"I don't know. I only heard the two shouting as I reported to the lab. When they saw me, they both went quiet. When I asked the doctor if he wanted me to report back to the Major General instead, he all but threatened me and sent me on my way."

"Yikes," Stansfield grimaced. "I wouldn't bother reading too much into that. He's probably under pressure the same as Dale—the same as I will be once I report to his office."

"I'm on my way there now. Care to join me."

"No, I'm gonna take a minute to update myself. How far along are we?"

"I don't share the major's confidence we might finish before the week is up. I didn't share that opinion with him, of course."

"Of course," she sighed. "Okay, tell Dale I'm on my way presently. And tell him I look like shit—how I'm ready to fight anyone who looks at me wrong. Maybe that'll convince him not to share the wealth when I get there."

JoAnne arrived in the corridor outside the Major General's office just as three gunshots rang out. She screamed and dropped to her knees in panic.

"Major?! Are you okay?"

When no answer came, JoAnne rose to her feet and slowly advanced to peer through the open office door.

The room was in disarray: a chair was overturned; files and books were scattered around the room. Lying on the ground before JoAnne and surrounded by spatters of fresh blood was Lieutenant Reimer.

"Aaron?" she whimpered.

The young man's eyes were lifeless, but they appeared somehow angry.

At the far end corner of the room stood the major general, his sidearm in his hand. He shook badly and only relaxed his grip when JoAnne called again.

"Major? What have you done?"

December 28th

JoAnne arrived at Anissa's office the next morning to find Staff Sergeant James Ostermann waiting beside her.

"Thank you for coming in, JoAnne," Stansfield said. She looked less worn now than she did yesterday morning, but there was clearly a weight on her shoulders that suppressed any warmth. "Sit down, please. Sergeant Ostermann has more questions."

"I apologize for pulling you back in here, Airman Harris," the man said somberly, "but additional information has come up, and I want to review some points with you again."

"I don't mind," JoAnne answered. "Frankly, I was tired of being alone and was going to come to see the technical sergeant, anyway. What would you like to know?"

"Thank you. Let's start by what reviewing what Major General Caroe said to you when you arrived at his office."

"All right."

"When you entered the room, you say you saw Lieutenant Reimer dead on the floor, and Major General Caroe standing over him pointing his side-arm at his body. Is that correct?"

"The major was standing across the room near the far left corner from the door. But yes, he was holding his side-arm."

"You heard Major General Caroe discharge the weapon moments earlier?"

"Yes, I heard it fire three times in rapid succession. I heard this from the hall just outside his office door."

"Did you hear anything that went on between the two men before you heard the gunshots?"

"No, sir. My mind was elsewhere as I was walking, and the gunfire startled me back to the present."

"What did the Major General say to you?" Ostermann asked, lowering his voice.

"I asked him what he'd done, and the major said that Lieutenant Reimer was going to kill him. He said the lieutenant had pushed into the room without knocking and tore the room up. 'Where is it?' was the

47

only thing Reimer said. The major said the lieutenant was deranged, and he that ordered Reimer to stop, but that he wouldn't. Then the major stood up and backed away from the desk to pull his side-arm. It was holstered on his belt, hanging with his jacket on the coat rack in the corner. Major Caroe said he then turned back and fired as the lieutenant was closing on him."

JoAnne paused, seeing in her mind the major's frightened face upon entering his office. She'd never seen the man resemble anything less than the edge of impatience in her life.

"Moments later, others arrived on the scene and disarmed the major," she continued. "I was escorted away. Then you and I discussed the matter an hour later."

"There were several bruises over Lieutenant Reimer's arms and chest. Some even on his neck and face. Did you notice them?"

"No, I didn't notice them."

"They appeared to be fresh—dark purple and green. You're sure you didn't notice them?"

"Honestly, I only looked at Aaron for a second. I was focused on the major and the gun in his hand."

"Okay, then. Let's go over some other points. Is it true that you accompanied Major General Caroe to Doctor Busch's lab two days ago on the morning of the twenty-sixth?"

"That's correct."

"What did the two men discuss during that meeting?"

"The major was unhappy to be called back from the Christmas break. We all were, of course. And he wanted the doctor to tell him how long the rest of the operation would take."

"The movement of the remaining storage boxes on Sub-Level Two?"

"That's right," she confirmed. "We've been done with Level 1 since the middle of the month. The major had told me he expected to be granted a reprieve from the deadline ordered by Lieutenant General Glinatsis. Instead, we received orders to cancel the holiday week and recall everyone on the twenty-sixth. We were to remain at work until

49

we completed the job. The major felt the doctor's inefficient management was the reason we had not finished in time."

"How did the doctor react to the major's remarks?"

"He was frustrated, but he was far calmer than the major. Ultimately, the Doctor Busch asked for help, and that's how I got assigned to assist him with cataloging."

"Which you did alongside the doctor and Sergeant Reimer?"

"That's correct."

"Did you ever notice Sergeant Reimer do anything suspicious while you were working alongside him?"

"No, not while we were working together."

Ostermann drew a breath to ask his next question, but stopped himself.

"Did you notice anything suspicious about him at any other time?"

JoAnne didn't answer, but averted her eyes from the lieutenant.

"Miss Harris?"

"I... I heard him having an argument yesterday morning."

"Who did the lieutenant argue with?" Ostermann asked, his face sharpening.

"With Doctor Busch."

"What time was this?"

"At zero-seven-hundred hours, when I reported to the lab to start the day's assignment."

"What did they argue about?"

"I don't know," JoAnne said.

"You don't know what the argument was about?"

"No, sir."

"Then how do you know they were arguing?"

"They were shouting at each other."

"What were they shouting?"

"I'm not sure," she shook her head. "I didn't hear much of it. I didn't even realize it was happening until I came around the corner onto Corridor L1-F. But when I arrived at the door, they saw me and stopped. Then Lieutenant Reimer left immediately."

"And you never talked to him after?"

"I never saw the lieutenant until the next morning in the major's office after he'd been shot dead."

"Did you speak to the doctor about the argument?"

"I asked if everything was okay, but he didn't answer me."

"You say you don't know what they argued about, but you must have heard something. What words did you hear?"

JoAnne shook her head with a defiant plea. She looked to Stansfield, uncertain of what to say, but the technical sergeant only nodded that JoAnne should continue.

"The only thing I can remember was that Lieutenant Reimer insisted he needed to get something—to do something—something the doctor had started. He demanded the doctor not turn his back on him. Then the doctor whispered something I barely heard. I think he told him to go wait for him somewhere."

Minutes passed after Ostermann finished the interview and left Stansfield's office before either woman said anything to each other.

"What do you think?" JoAnne finally asked.

"I can't believe you said that," Stansfield answered after shaking her head for several moments.

"What do you mean?"

"Why would you throw Ian under the bus like that? I mean, I realize he upset you, but to make it seem like he was withholding something... Do you realize what you've done?"

"I didn't exaggerate that part, Anissa. That's what Aaron said just before he saw me and stopped shouting."

"What did he say exactly?"

"Something like, 'You started this.'"

"Something like that? You don't remember the exact words?" Stansfield's expression darkened.

"Well, no. I don't remember the exact words."

"But you just told Ostermann like you knew for certain what he said. What were you thinking? What if you didn't hear him correctly?"

"I know what he was trying to say," JoAnne insisted. "Just because I can't remember the words verbatim... They were shouting at the top of their lungs. Do you think I imagined that?"

Stansfield exhaled with frustration.

"Fine. You might as well go back to the barracks and rest."

"I'm not going back there. To do what? Sit around and stare at the walls?"

"All right, fine," Stansfield looked at JoAnne with impatience. "Your orders are to return to your duties with Doctor Busch. I expect he may be busy with Ostermann defending himself from your accusations, but that shouldn't take too long. Go ahead back to the lab and wait for him to finish. Then work with the doctor to finish cataloging the restricted materials."

JoAnne was speechless.

It took an hour before Doctor Busch finished his second interview with Ostermann in the laboratory. When the staff sergeant had finally left the room, JoAnne entered to find the doctor silent in thought. He seemed surprised to see her there when he finally noticed that he wasn't alone. But the emotion quickly turned into a light smile.

"You're kidding," Busch said incredulously.

"Technical Sergeant Stansfield has ordered me to offer my help to complete L2-13."

"Did she? And you're okay with that?"

"It's fine," JoAnne acknowledge without offering more. "Shall we resume?"

The doctor didn't answer immediately, staring at JoAnne in disbelief.

"Very well, then."

Busch led the way back downstairs without a word, moving straight through the dim halls and corridors at a reasonable pace. For the first time, she felt confident she could get back upstairs without guessing.

When they arrived at the room, JoAnne looked back down the corridor. She remembered how Aaron Reimer had caught up with them that first time, making her grateful there would be three working on the room together. She didn't have the nerve to comment on that feeling now. Instead, she entered into the warm glow of L2-13, ready for what awaited her.

Despite her reservations, Doctor Busch went right back to work. With a crowbar, he opened each crate and described its contents to JoAnne. In turn, she quoted the manifest, and if the doctor agreed, she retyped the information into a new form. If he wanted a slightly different description, JoAnne would accommodate. If the contents were not what the manifest described, she would note the difference in her update.

JoAnne and Doctor Busch worked in this manner for hours, only breaking once, when she briefly visited the mess hall for lunch.

Around 15:00 hours, the doctor stopped and sat down on a crate, clearly exhausted.

JoAnne didn't care to sit next to the man, but her feet were painfully sore from standing all day.

"Have a seat," he offered, nodding to a crate on the opposite side of the aisle.

With a silent sigh, JoAnne sat down, grateful as the pain in her feet slowly lessened.

"I suppose I owe you an apology," Busch said after a moment. "I was impatient with you yesterday. You were only trying to be helpful."

JoAnne shook her head as if it didn't matter.

"It's fine, Doctor."

"At the time, I presumed you heard all of my argument with the lieutenant. But based on what you reported during Ostermann's interview, you only heard the last bit."

"It was none of my business, Doctor," JoAnne shook her head again.

"Reimer had sought my assistance. He had a problem with Dale, and he thought that I would support him because Dale and I aren't exactly close. But the truth is that I respect Dale a great deal, and I didn't agree with anything Aaron proposed, which angered him. Now looking back, I understand that Aaron wasn't well."

Busch exhaled deeply and shook his head.

"I was angered by the suggestion, even if part of me believed it. Perhaps that's why it upset me so much. And when you spoke up, just trying to be helpful, I took that anger out on you for no reason. Please, forgive me."

She'd be lying to say the doctor's admission didn't surprise her. JoAnne was unaccustomed to apologies coming from anyone in this place, especially people at the top.

"Apology accepted, Doctor. Don't give it another thought," she nodded.

From overhead, they heard a massive impact. Something shook the roof.

"Was that an explosion?" JoAnne asked.

"We'd better move."

They left their work behind and hurried to the door. In the hallway, Busch pulled his keys out to lock up the secured room.

From somewhere down the corridor and around the corner, gunfire rang out. JoAnne starred into the dim light.

"I don't think we should go back that way, doctor."

Looking back at Busch for a response, she found him staring at her. In his right hand, he held the packing mallet. Before she could say anything, he struck her in the head.

December 29th

JoAnne's eyes opened to the sound of distant gunfire, but she saw nothing. Instead, she was in darkness, greeted only by a terrible, almost paralyzing pain. It took the young woman time to sit up and realize she was in a tightly confined space. Reaching out to feel the walls, she soon noticed the faint light glowing around the door frame. It anchored JoAnne's mind, and she used it to guide her intuitively to the light switch on the wall.

JoAnne found herself standing in a storage closet, surrounded by janitorial supplies. Reaching for the doorknob, she discovered it was locked from the outside.

"Hello? Is someone there?"

Without thinking, JoAnne beat on the door with her palms and called for help.

From down the corridor, she heard quiet steps approaching. Then came the sound of a woman breathing in a panic.

"Hello?" JoAnne called again.

A quiet gasp sounded, and both the footsteps and breathing abruptly halted.

"Who's there?" she called again.

"JoAnne?" Tech Sergeant Stansfield answered.

"Anissa, is that you? Can you open the door? I think it's locked."

"What do you mean? Who locked you in there?"

"I'm not sure," JoAnne said without confidence. "My head is pounding. I must've blacked out and hit it on something…"

Through the pain, JoAnne saw Doctor Busch's face flash in her memory. His eyes; the mallet in his hands.

"I think the doctor put me inside here."

"Maybe he was trying to keep you hidden?" Stansfield whispered. Her voice sounded terrified.

"Hide me from what?"

"It's gone to hell upstairs. Lieutenant Ostermann has gone insane. I radioed Security for backup, but I didn't get a response. Then I fled for cover."

"What do you mean, insane?"

"He's shot at least seven people. We tried to engage him, but he won't speak to us. His eyes… Ostermann looks deranged. The skin on his hands and face have horrible welts like someone beat him savagely. He's shot so many people dead. Even after we rose to attention, we still couldn't stop him. I managed to get him once in the leg, but it only slowed him down. I think he's on some sort of methamphetamine or something."

"Like Aaron? Isn't that how he described Lieutenant Reimer before he shot him?

"I don't know—maybe. Do you have a weapon on you?"

"No," JoAnne said, looking around her. "There's cleaning only supplies in here. I have a broomstick."

"Well, keep that handy. Stay there for now, and be quiet. You're probably safe in there if he doesn't know about it. I'll come back for you when this is—"

Something crashed in the distance, and Stansfield went silent. Moments later, JoAnne screamed at the sound of two shots firing outside the closet door from Stansfield's gun.

"Anissa?"

From down the corridor, the furious stride of heavy footsteps echoed toward them. Anissa gasped awkwardly and fled in response. JoAnne instinctively stepped back from the door as the pounding footsteps raced past her.

From only twenty paces away, Anissa's voice cried out. It was not the sound of fear—she was in agony. A chilling sound of ripping preceded a gurgling that soon overcame Anissa's voice, and all that followed was silence.

JoAnne startled herself and realized that the sound coming from her feet was on account of her right leg shaking uncontrollably.

Be still, she told herself.

The quieter JoAnne became, the more her racing heartbeat pounded in her ears. Realizing the closet lightbulb might shine around the doorframe, she reached to flip the switch off. She hardly made a sound, but it only took moments to realize her error.

The heavy steps advanced slowly down the corridor to the closet, and finding it locked, their owner grabbed the knob to shake it violently. Then JoAnne heard the peculiar sound of erratic sniffing, like a dog searching, which raised the hairs on her neck. In the dark, she saw a moving shadow, presumably Ostermann, on the other side of the door. He seemed to smell her through the seams of the doorframe.

A sharp impact rattled the door loudly, drawing a startled gasp from JoAnne. He undoubtedly heard her and slapped his fists wildly against the door, pausing only to use his shoulder in a feeble try to break inward the outward-opening door.

A strangled growl of frustrated anger rose as the violent pounding intensified. Ostermann's animalistic grunting horrified JoAnne more than anything, and she held to the wall to keep from falling down as her legs weakened.

Another gunshot rang out, and again she screamed. But to JoAnne's relief, Ostermann seemed incapacitated or dead. His heavy frame slumped to the ground against the door.

"Anissa?" she repeatedly called in vain, desperate to know that the tech sergeant was still alive.

JoAnne sensed indistinct movement and reached to flip the closet light switch again. The slumped body seemed to move, but she was certain Ostermann was being dragged away rather than moving by his own will.

She exhaled at the sound of a key sliding into the lock with relief. When the door opened, JoAnne saw Doctor Busch standing alone. He held a gun in his hand.

"You're safe for now. Come with me."

As JoAnne and Doctor Busch moved through Sub-Level B to the stairs, they came across at least thirteen dead bodies. The gruesome sight cleared JoAnne's mind despite the terrible throbbing in her head. She understood the doctor would likely kill her. Though JoAnne's eyes raced to find any opportunity for escape, any weapon to defend herself with, the gun pointed at her back rendered such notions pointless.

"Inside that room," Busch gestured with his pistol when they arrived at his laboratory.

Past his desk were three doors, the center of which bore a small, one-by-one square foot window with chicken wire running through two panes of glass. She'd never noticed it before, thinking all three were storage closets, but it appeared to be a holding cell for patients. An occupant could easily see through the window but couldn't reach to unlock the door by merely shattering the glass. Below it appeared to be a large mail slot JoAnne figured was for passing meals through.

JoAnne unlatched the lock and pulled the door open. Inside, the room was padded with a soft, white spongy material from floor to ceiling, including the door's inside. There was a single twin bed in one corner and a toilet on the opposite side.

JoAnne felt a sudden acute sense of claustrophobia, and she turned back to the doctor with undisguised fear.

"Please don't put me in here," she pleaded quietly, her chin trembling.

He exhaled deeply, but it wasn't impatience that drove him.

"You have my word—it'll only be for a short while. Look here, I'll keep this slot open the whole time, and I won't turn the light off. I promise."

He gently closed the door and opened the slot as he promised.

"There. You can hear me just fine, can't you? There's no way you could run out of air. You can see me well enough, right?"

JoAnne began to cry, but she nodded.

"In fact, we'll both be out of here in fifteen minutes. We're going to drive out together. But first things first."

The doctor went to one of the worktables against the room's perimeter and pulled open a storage cabinet door. From within, he pulled two glass bottles, one small and one considerably larger. From a drawer at his waist, he took a small syringe and drew a small amount of liquid. Then the doctor turned the needle up, flicked at the glass with his index finger, and shot out a brief stream of liquid. He retrieved two cotton balls out of a large glass container on the counter and wet one with the larger bottle's liquid.

"I am going to give you an injection that will help calm you and give you the clarity and strength you'll need for our trip."

JoAnne instinctively withdrew from the door.

Doctor Busch nodded with appreciation.

"I understand your apprehension, but let me make myself clear. One way or another, I'm going to administer this shot. Now, you can either extend your arm out for me willingly, or I'll release gas into the room that'll knock you out, then make the injection while you're unconscious. I promise the first choice is much less challenging for us both."

Visions of suffocating in the room while clouds of gas overtook JoAnne's imagination. The fear prompted her to roll up her uniform shirt sleeve and slowly extended her arm through the slot in response.

"Good. There, you're very trim—I can see a vein."

He wiped at the crook of JoAnne's arm with the wet cotton ball, then placed his index finger on her skin and slid the needle gently into the skin. She felt the sting, but it lasted only a few seconds before he withdrew it. Finally, he placed the dry cotton ball at the puncture.

"Hold this there and close your arm for a few minutes while it clots."

The doctor returned to the table and dropped the syringe into a box marked Used. He then walked across the room to another counter where two small wooden crates lay open. Both were marked TOP SECRET—U.S. Air Force and clearly came from Room L2-13.

"What's in those?" she asked.

Busch turned back to her for a moment and smiled.

"We don't really know," he admitted. "One of them contains rocks from an unknown origin. And the other contains… mechanical parts."

"From a plane?"

"No, definitely not from a plane. We've seen nothing like them. All of this was found at a crash site north of here years ago."

"But they're not from the plane that crashed?"

"No, it wasn't a plane that crashed. We don't know what it was, only that it was a machine of some sort."

"Foreign? Russian?" JoAnne asked.

"We transported most of it out of here shortly after retrieving it, but I managed to keep these under my nose. The rocks are inert unless combined with fluorine, then they produce a psychotropic compound. My research has proven the machine parts are made from an unknown material. Some parts are forged without the slightest seam, which is well beyond what we're capable of."

He replaced the lids and reached for a mallet and nails.

"Or the Russians, to answer your question," he added.

When he'd sealed them, Busch lifted both crates and placed them on a trolley.

"I'll be back in ten minutes for you. Have a seat and rest, if you can."

"Doctor, why did you tell me about the content of those boxes?"

Busch stopped and turned back.

"It won't matter, dear."

With that, he pushed the trolley out of the laboratory and walked away.

JoAnne dropped her arm from its crooked position and pulled off the cotton ball to see the injection point. A dark purple and green bruise had already appeared at the injection, spread three inches from the hole. She gasped in terror and choked, which sent her into fits of coughing before he could calm her breathing.

In time, JoAnne worked up the courage to touch the bruise. To her surprise, it didn't hurt. The needle puncture was tender, but otherwise, she couldn't feel the bruise. But then she felt slightly dizzy and put her hand out onto the wall to steady herself.

They were small shifts in JoAnne's vision that came in waves, and she moved to the bed to sit down. Almost missing the edge, she fell back on the bed and gripped the sides. It felt as if the room was moving and that she might roll off the bed to the ground.

Each time the spinning slowed, JoAnne's head would pound painfully. Her ears began to ring, the sound expanding each time the spinning resumed.

That son of a bitch, she thought. Anger overtook JoAnne's fear. He'd betrayed her; injected her with some poison to no doubt keep her submissive.

Resistant, JoAnne swung her legs around and attempted to sit up, refusing to give in. She wouldn't go with him—she wouldn't become a hostage.

When the room slowed, she stood up successfully. The spinning only returned once, and she gripped hold of the door slot to keep her balance. When it finally stopped, she slapped the wall loudly in defiance, satisfied to have prevailed.

JoAnne's eye caught the skin on her forearm arm. Another bruise had appeared, dark and unsightly.

"Goddamn it!" she screamed.

No sooner had she caught her breath than she heard Doctor Busch's footsteps down the corridor outside the laboratory door.

"How are you feeling?" he asked when he'd made it back to the holding cell door.

"What the hell have you done to me? What was that injection?"

"It's nothing. Just something to calm you," he said.

"It's not working."

Doctor Busch stared at her silently for a moment, as if examining her eyes and her body's movements.

"I believe it is. So, it's time to go. Now," he said, pulling his pistol from the holster inside his white coat, "I'm going to let you out of there. You should make for the southern service entrance. There are two guards there, and they will help you. And if you don't like the effects of that sedative, they have an antidote in their office they can administer."

His proposal— escaping—flooded JoAnne's stunned mind.

"Do you mean it? You'll let me go?"

"Absolutely. It's only a quarter-mile walk. If you hurry, you can be there in five minutes. Are you ready?"

JoAnne breathed heavily in anticipation of the door opening, of running as fast as she could to be free to find the antidote that awaited her.

Bush placed his hand on the door but stopped, turning his head.

"What is it? Please," she pleaded.

Busch looked back at JoAnne with dead eyes and sighed.

From the corridor outside the laboratory, she heard several heavy footsteps approaching. Busch lifted the gun before they entered the room, placed the end in his mouth, and pulled the trigger.

JoAnne screamed in shock and fell back to the floor. She quickly got back to her feet and found the laboratory had filled with half a dozen men, all armed and prepared for what might await them. When they seemed satisfied that the room was secure, Major Caroe entered from behind them.

"Dale!" she screamed, overcome by gratitude and relief.

Caroe rushed to the holding room and stopped at the doctor's body on the ground.

"Move this man to the side at once," he ordered the other airmen.

Two men leaped into action, collectively repositioning Busch's corpse out of the door's path. Caroe placed his hand on the door lock impatiently.

"Don't worry, Harris. We're going to get you out of there in just—"

Caroe's words caught in his throat when he saw JoAnne's face up close through the wired glass.

"Please, sir. I have to get out of this little room. It was the doctor—all of it was his fault. He did something to Ostermann—gave him something that made him crazy. Ostermann killed everyone but the doctor and me," she said in a rabid frenzy, straining to stare down at Busch's feet.

"He wanted to steal something from the restricted room," she continued. "He was preparing to leave with two top-secret crates while

74

no one was around to stop him. He was just about to let me go. He said the guards at the south gate could help me. He gave me a sedative to calm me down, and—"

JoAnne stared down at her arm, pulling back the fabric of her open sleeve to look at the injection. The original bruise had spread. Its ugly dark purple and green splotches now appeared all the way to her wrist.

The door slot slammed closed, startling JoAnne. Dale had slid it shut to lock.

"Sir? Please, I don't want to be in here. I don't feel well—my head is spinning from where he knocked me out."

Caroe only stared at her through the glass.

"Major, please, I'm afraid. Can't you see? I'm having a bad reaction to the sedative he gave me. He said the guards at the south gate could help me. They have an antidote to stop it. Look," she held out her arm for him to see, "look at how allergic I am to it."

Caroe's expression was grave as he stared at her eyes. He stepped back from the door several paces and turned his back to speak with one of the men in the room. This other man immediately looked up at JoAnne over the short distance with great tension and shook his head.

"Major, what are you doing? I said I need you to let me out of here."

Neither man stopped their conversation.

"Major, I said to let me out! Major! Dale!" JoAnne yelled, and she slapped the door.

She breathed heavily, annoyed with his rude insensitivity. Why was the son of a bitch always acting that way? JoAnne had put up with it for years; they all had. But now, when she needed his help, he couldn't even be bothered to hurry.

"Goddamn it, let me out of here now! Dale! Dale!!!"

Caroe looked back from across at the glass briefly, but soon resumed his conversation with the other man.

"You MOTHERFUCKER!" JoAnne screamed at the top of her lungs. "Open this door!"

Her raging voice overcame her, and she placed her hands on her head, which pounded relentlessly. She swayed backward but caught herself and fought the sensation off. JoAnn wouldn't let it deter her.

When she looked up, one of the other men stood beside the door, unlatching the lock. From where Caroe stood, he nodded to the man, who opened the door swiftly and stood back.

"Dale," she whimpered to see him raise his gun.

With a loud bang that echoed slowly, the lights in the room darkened. JoAnne couldn't hear for several long moments before the sound stopped.

Then there was nothing at all…

THERE ARE PEOPLE
BY THOMAS FUCALORO

There are people

who are worried

about aliens

and an alien's religious belief.

They want to add more

unknown to the unknown

so it can all disappear

into this one cosmic

illusion called

the answer.

I often think if there is a god

it's an alien or something

outer space,

something undiscovered.

I wonder if god

finds us alien

in our beliefs?

Will the space-alien-lizard-pterodactyl-people with twelve arms

quote us scripture from all the testaments claimed

or will they just eat us all the same?

I get nervous when what we don't know

becomes armed

with more of what we don't know.

I believe in people and their beliefs

but I don't believe in people

who have the answer

because the answer

usually leads to the defending of

and that can lead to hate and violence

and understanding becomes something

we only whisper to ourselves.

Whenever these things or creatures or light or beings

decide to enter this world I think our beliefs might

have to take a rest for a day or 2. When the unknown

 arrives you need to start taking questions for answers

and realize that believing

in something

anything

might only be

a human function.

THE ROSWELL STORY
BY LAUREN ALEXIS WOOD

"Smith! Johnson! In my office! Now!"

Commander Esilas was known for his anger issues. The man was in his late thirties but the constant stress of his position had taken its toll. His receding hairline, expanding waistline and constant forced frown added at least a decade to his appearance. His dingy, windowless office on the lower-level of the Pentagon was somewhat of a prison. His job, somewhat of a joke. His only function after being a once highly-decorated commanding officer in the field had been reduced to fielding incoming complaints on governmental agency missteps and classified project slip-ups, then being tasked with coordinating cover-ups or drumming up alternative press. Day-to-day the amount of nonsense that crossed his desk was enough to give any reasonable person an ulcer, however this time, things were beyond just a simple mishap.

Truth be told, the events of last night's incident were enough to enrage the most level-headed officer in any command.

"A goddamn rancher found the debris from one of the Project Mogul prototypes at a crash site on his property and has already contacted the media. I need you two in Roswell, New Mexico. Tomorrow. I need you two to get this thing under control. The true details of this project can NOT reach the public. Not now. Not like this. You need to put together an alternative explanation and you need to do it tonight."

"Project Mogul? Is that the top-secret "weather balloon" thing?" Smith questioned while making air quotes.

Johnson chuckled at his partner's nonchalance.

Officers Smith and Johnson were routinely called in to coordinate and oversee damage control for top-secret, first-line classified government programs around the United States. Simple mistakes often snowballed when left to the unpredictable nature of public speculation and their professional partnership was based on their expert ability to craft convincing and airtight alternative explanations for government mistakes, from the simplest of oversights to major disasters.

Project Mogul was a program headquartered at a top secret location within an East Coast University system.

The project used Roswell and other Southwestern airfields to test the durability and feasibility of an undetectable aircraft meant to travel in the upper atmosphere where it was theorized that sound waves traveled similarly to their passage in water. The Air Force and Navy were partnered on the project and the technology would eventually be refined in order to monitor Soviet nuclear testing activity from afar. Most recently the prototypes had been inspired by weather balloon technology borrowed from NARL and futuristic design ideas submitted by interns at NASA.

"This isn't simply a PR concern!" the commander bellowed while pacing his office. Smith and Johnson sat calmly on the leather couch in the corner.

Everyone knew that letting the Commander vent while actively in crisis was usually the best option.

"Son of a bitch! This concerns National safety! If word spreads that we are testing technology to better monitor Soviet activity the public panic that could erupt would be unmanageable. I need a briefing from you both on your plan by oh nineteen hundred and I want you on a plane by 6am tomorrow to New Mexico. Now, out of my office!"

Great. Just… great.

A wrecked experimental research craft in rural New Mexico? What were they doing at Alamogordo?!

The government's involvement was obvious. People would have questions regarding the nature of the aircraft and the details of this project remained confidential. The public speculation could put everything, and everyone involved in Project Mogul, in compromise.

"Johnson, what if we told them it was a new material we are testing for futuristic spacecraft and we had to test its resilience in a simulated launch that failed?" Smith suggested as the two sat shoulder-to-shoulder in the basement breakroom of the Pentagon, each facing a legal pad with scribbled notes and failed ideas.

"I don't think they're going to buy it." Smith countered. "According to the intel we have, the rancher fully examined the crash site. There isn't anything there to back up that claim. Tin foil. A basic radar unit. Rubber. Give me something else."

"I've got nothing! Tell me you have something in that chicken scratch." Johnson argued, motioning to Smith's legal pad scribblings.

"What about an experimental crop-dusting aircraft? Or debris from something like that?" Smith offered.

"That doesn't make any sense. The rancher would be in charge of his own field." Johnson sighed while scribbling out a line of his own handwriting.

As the two sat in intense thought, the interior phone on the wall across the room began to ring.

"Twenty dollars says that's the Commander with demands on our strategy for this." Smith offered as Johnson crossed the room to answer.

"I'll give you five. We both know it's him."

As Johnson picked up the line, the sounds of Commander Esilas' verbal abuse filled the silent room through the mouthpiece of the phone. Johnson put his hand over the receiver to mute his voice.

"Smith, we have to tell him something. What do you have? Give me an idea!"

"Uh……. um…… aliens! Tell him that we'll explain to the simple people of Roswell, New Mexico that it's an extraterrestrial spacecraft that visitors from another planet crash-landed while attempting to make contact with the people of Earth. We'll tell them we are aware of the magnitude of this historic event and that the government has the situation completely under control."

Johnson blinked incredulously, his hand still over the receiver. "That's honestly the dumbest thing I have ever heard come out of your mouth. It's… genius."

As Johnson explained the plan to the Commander the yells from the other end of the line slowly silenced.

"Yes, sir. Correct. Yes. The people of Roswell, New Mexico are a simple folk. Yes. The population of Rural New Mexico is naive and easily persuaded. Yes, this is ridiculous enough to work. Okay. Yes, we're both on the first flight out of DCA tomorrow. Yes. That's right. Mmm-hmm. Correct. Yes, Commander. Okay."

Johnson hung up the phone and turned to Smith, who'd already stood up, gathered his things and appeared ready to leave the room.

"Aliens?" Johnson questioned.

"Aliens." Smith confirmed.

.   .   .

Their flights were fairly uneventful.

Between the two of them they had smuggled enough hard liquor into the plane to tranquilize them both for the cross-country journey. However, their layover in Dallas would be the perfect time to get their story airtight before touching down in New Mexico.

The 200 mile drive from Albuquerque to Roswell would be filled with brainstorming a strategy on how to reach media outlets to try to get ahead of the rumors started by the rancher and other townsfolk. A news team had already gotten footage and a live interview with the story was to air that night on the local six o' clock news. The local paper was planning a cover story the next morning. In a last-ditch effort they had to at least make an attempt to try to stall the debut or try to convince them not to release the exclusive story in exchange for an official Government statement on extraterrestrials.

They'd also contacted the farm where the wreckage was found and were planning on meeting the rancher and his family at 3pm local time near the crash site to attempt an explanation and cover-up of the true nature of Project Mogul.

"Do you think these people are going to speak English or...?" Smith asked as the two agents sat at a bar in their terminal awaiting their next flight in Dallas.

"It's NEW Mexico. Of course they speak English." Johnson quipped back.

"No, I know. I know they *technically* speak English, but is it going to be understandable? Remember the radioactive containers that fell off that truck in rural Nevada during tha..."

"That was a fucking. Nightmare. Also, those people were Indians. American Indians. They had their own dialect a..."

"You don't think some podunk rancher in rural New Mexico isn't going to have his own dialect? We aren't going to be able to understand these fucking people. The town is up in arms because a rancher essentially found some garbage on his property that fell from the sky? I mean,

Jesus. Fucking. Christ. Did you even read the briefing and see the rough news footage intel sent us this morning? Unintelligible."

"Well fuck me then. I guess I'll have another beer."

As the two ordered one more round and made their way to their gate Johnson checked his carry on only to find a written note from Commander Esilas.

Do NOT fuck this up. I'm counting on you two. The entirety of National Security is counting on you.

"Goddammit." Johnson muttered.

""Encouragement" from Esilas?" Smith asked, making air quotes.

"Yeah."

.   .   .

"Jesus Christ! This car was a poor choice."

As the two made their way through the New Mexican landscape, the gravel and dust pelted the underside of their Ford. It was a 35 minute drive to the crash site from Roswell city-center and the rutted road had obviously not seen much traffic. They'd secured a vehicle at the airport through the Air Force but the car was not equipped for speed, much less any significant distance on anything other than pavement.

"Do you think the alien thing is too much?" Smith questioned.

"Please don't backpedal on this now. It's too late. We've already committed to this backstory and we need to see it through. Not one other idea of ours has demonstrated that it has a leg to stand on. This explains everything and takes care of any public speculation on the origins of the craft."

"Yeah, but do you think that this could get blown out of proportion? Do you think that this has the potential to be worse? Aliens from another planet? Really?"

"Don't be stupid. Oh! Look! There's the ranch!"

As they made their way around a bend in the road a farmhouse appeared on the left. As they drove alongside the fence running along the property line against the road, several farm dogs barked and playfully ran alongside the vehicle.

As the agents pulled into the gravel driveway the rancher, his wife and a handful of children walked from the front porch of the farmhouse to meet them. The agents gave each other a knowing glance before exiting the vehicle.

"I reckon you two gentlemen are from the Government?" the rancher stated, the moment the car doors had closed.

The mid afternoon sun beat down on them, the dust kicked up into the air and clung to the sweat already forming on the agents' faces.

"Jesus Christ it must be a hundred degrees out here!" Johnson exclaimed.

"It's eighty five according to my weather vane. Tell me, are you the two gentlemen from the US Government?" the rancher pressed.

"Yes. Yes sir. We are Government agents." Smith answered.

The rancher's wife clutched her youngest child tighter and several of the children began to whisper amongst themselves.

"There's absolutely no need for alarm. We are simply here to examine the crash site. The alien spacecraft crash si…" Johnson planted the seed.

"Excuse me, did you say alien spacecraft? Alien, like, outer space aliens?" the rancher's wife blurted out.

"Honey, please keep your voice down and let the men speak. Why don't you go inside and check on the pies?" the rancher scolded.

As his wife gathered her children and started walking back toward the house she glanced back at the agents with an equal mixture of fear and curiosity.

The rancher turned to the agents. "Do you mean to tell me the wreckage on my property is from outer space?"

"Yessir. An extremely advanced and intelligent race from Planet…" Johnson trailed off slightly, forgetting the backstory briefing they'd been rehearsing all morning.

"From Planet RU-176." Smith jumped in with the assist. "This is an alien race that has decided to make contact with the people of Earth. We have the beings in custody, we just haven't a chance to clean the wreckage. We truly appreciate your patience and we hope to get this cleaned up right away. I understand you've contacted some news outlets, however, if you could keep this quiet that would be amazing."

"Uh… sure. I can do that." the rancher replied.

TRIP OF A LIFETIME
BY MATTHEW HOWELS

The little Grey man took

A wrong turn and wound up

In Roswell. Poor fucker.

THE DIVIDE
BY BRUNE SMITH

There's the people 35 and under

and then there's those over 65

nothing in between

The Young ones die before their 36th birthday

and I swear

I saw a gray-haired couple smirk

holding hands

walking

slow and steady

fearless

joyful, even

robots, really

a slap in our Young faces

Saw them from the keyhole

of my last hiding place

We hide,

we're all nerves now

How they made it through those hollow years

was a mystery

to me

soon-to-be 33

until the Reveal

They are Other

Roswellian Syndrome
by Callahan Herrig

I found myself stumbling around the desert one night. It was only my first week in Roswell, New Mexico but the air was cool and my skin warm. Was it the weed I smoked, no… maybe it was the beer? Had to be… wait the LSD/Acid might have finally kicked in…that could be. Regardless, I shuffled through the desert with my LL Bean sheepherders jacket looking for something; myself? My feet continued to carry me. I had been flush with cash for a while since my last case but has finally dried up. Not a lot of work for a burnt-out private investigator but here we are. Am I out here hoping to find work? Doubtful. Something drew me out to this remote place.

There was a bright flash and several other lights some yards ahead of me over the next hill. Did I really see something or was it the drugs? I climbed the hill on all fours, it seemed safer that way as I steadily made it to the top to peek over. As I crested the hill a unique site befell me.

Several objects were sticking out of the ground, half-submerged. Lots of bright lights and even more people in black suits, military uniforms, white lab coats, and hazmat suits were running around. Areas taped off, biohazard symbols everywhere, it was pure chaos. My eyes were wide with wonder taking it all in when they caught a glimpse of something. Several extremely tall individuals had hoods over their heads being put into the back of the van, their skin looked grey...but I couldn't be sure. As I leaned farther over the ridge, I heard a loud THUMP, and everything went dark...

When I came to, I was face to face with two waiters. No...wait, chauffeurs? They were wearing black suits, both looked oddly similar, and stared at me with intensity. I was in a chair across from them, in a nondescript room.

"I'll take a Reuben with a side of fries," I said to the men in black.

They looked at one another confused then turned back to me. "Do you know what you saw tonight, Mr. Coltrane?"

"Call me Slab, most do. How do you know my name?"

One pulled out my wallet and threw it back to me. That answered that question. "Mr. Coltrane, we ran a background check and know that you are a Private Investigator. Now, it is imperative that you tell us what it is you think you saw tonight."

"Frankly fellas...can I call you Frank? Frankly, I don't remember seeing anything, my head is fuzzy on account of the bump on the head I took."

The boys in suits were getting annoyed with my antics and one walked around my chair behind me. "Mr. Coltrane, we need to know what you think you might have seen. It is of utmost importance."

These boys were definitely government officials, bad haircuts, no dress sense, and an air of scumbag entitlement. I stared at the one in front of me and decided I needed to get out of here. "Listen, I was out camping in the desert, I wandered away from my campsite because I had a few too many beers and passed out. Next thing I knew I woke up here with you two."

The suit in front of me eyed his partner behind me. He motioned his finger across his nose and nodded. The suit behind me put his hand on my shoulder. "Listen, Mr. Coltrane, we appreciate your candor, so we are going to let you go. Before we do, you must take this." His other hand came over my shoulder holding what looked like a tab of LSD.

"What. What is that?" I feigned sincerity as I knew exactly what it was.

"This will help clear any cobwebs you might...have...and you probably won't remember this conversation." He then proceeded to open my mouth and threw the LSD down my throat.

I gulped it down and a bag went over my head.

Next thing I knew I woke up in my apartment that doubled as my office. It was an absolute mess, it looked like they tore the place apart looking for something. Actually, this is exactly how I left it before my trip into the desert...never mind. I think the suit gave me a bum tab, I still would've been tripping. Government officials never know good drugs from bad ones.

What had I witnessed in the last 12 hours? I've been in Roswell for less than a week and already I've stumbled upon some sort of government conspiracy. When I moved here for more cases, I never imagined something like this. What the hell did I see over that hill...those creatures, beings, beasts, those life forms? I really have to lay off the mind-altering substances for a while. Opening my fridge I grabbed my last beer and sat at the only chair at my kitchen table (card table) and took a swig.

Its turtles all the way down I thought to myself. Those boys in black knew I saw something, but what the hell did I even see? Why were they so pushy to know what I saw? This is heavy I thought as I took another long drink.

I'm still alive, I didn't end up in a bunker or a ditch somewhere. But where do I go from here? I have to go back to that gorge and see what really happened. How could I possibly find my way back to that exact spot?

My head was more cluttered than my apartment. Some food would do me good I thought. I'll make a stop at the only contact I have here in Roswell. An old friend who opened a diner here many moons ago. Goes by the name of Bill Pumpkin. Bill owns a diner in the middle of town called 'Pumpkin's Plate'. Aptly named because the special of the day was always Pumpkin's Plate, and it was a random dish that never had pumpkin in it.

I walked the 6 blocks to Bill's diner. Pushing the door open a bell dinged that signaled my entrance. Bill looked up from the fryer and gave me a nod and pointed to a seat at the bar. The place was empty save for a young couple sharing a milkshake in the corner. I slid into the seat at the bar and looked at the menu. It was 30 pages long.

"Really diversifying your menu aren't you there Bill?"

He flipped a couple of pancakes on the grill and turned around to me. "Blow it out your ass Slab. Most people don't get past the first 3 pages anyway. What's going on with you?"

I then proceeded to tell him about the long night I had. The desert, lights, life forms, and the men in black suits. His face seemed incredulous at first, but as I told the story he began nodding solemnly as if understanding. He was about to speak when the bell dinged singling someone entering the diner.

I turned to look and in walked the two agents in black suits that shook me down the night before. My eyes widened as they took a booth near the door and nodded to Bill. I turned to look at Bill, he had an uneasy look on his face. He gritted his teeth and walked over to the agents table to take their order.

He came back and started grilling up 2 "Pumpkin Plates" for the agents and turned back to me. We made small talk before he slid me a napkin that read, "Go the bathroom when I take out their orders. There is a window, get out of here, they're tailing you."

103

I looked up from the napkin and Bill winked at me as he grabbed the napkin and threw it into the trash can. Of course these suits came in now, I was starving and never got my Pumpkin Plate. I tried to look casual as Bill took the agents their plates. I got up slowly and went to the bathroom. I caught their eyes tracking me but went back to their food as they saw I went to the john.

Locking the door, I locate the window and pop it open. I slip outside into the desert heat and sprint back to my apartment. Bill bought me some precious minutes, so I need to take advantage. I grabbed my car keys and a jacket and decided I need to try and find that gorge again. My car was a beater and low on gas. I hopped in and sped out onto the highway to find the exit.

I found the exit I took that night, Exit 69, I only remember that because I laughed when I took it. I drove about 2 miles off the exit and parked the car, dust settling. I look around for familiar landmarks and thinking a hill in the distance looked familiar. I climbed the hill on all fours like I had before, finally arriving to the top. Once I reached the top I looked over into a deep gorge.

Nothing was there. It was an empty gorge. No tire tracks, no lab coats, an empty gorge. I sat down on the top of the hill confused and frankly lost.

What the hell is going on I thought...

I took a tab of LSD out of my pocket and placed it on my tongue. I swallowed and laid down on the top of the hill slowly fading in and out of consciousness.

I awoke to find the two men in black standing over me. Their faces looked like galaxies on account of the drugs.

"Mr. Coltrane, you need to come with us. Now."

"Do I know you fellas?" I replied slurring my words.

They slipped a bag over my head and dragged me into a black van. The next few hours were extremely hazy. I awoke in my apartment once again, this time it was spotless clean.

"WHAT IS GOING ON" I shouted alone in my apartment.

A knock at my door brought me back to reality. I opened the door and a beautiful woman stood there with a stern look on her face.

"You don't know me Mr. Coltrane… but I got your name from Bill Pumpkin. He said you were a Private Investigator and you take on cases. It sounds crazy but I need someone to look into it. It involves extraterrestrial beings."

I let out a sigh, "Sure, please step into my office."

She walked in and I closed the door behind her.

CIVIL WAR IN SPACE
BY JUSTIN FOYIL

Circumcise the human

and bring it to rare form,

this is what you will see

when your life hits the light.

The rarest chances

then become composed,

when you allow external life

to be exposed.

We are not them,

we are but circumstance

wishing to be unique, the different, always...

searching for extra-terrestrial emotion,

and our lives to advance.

We all are not human

but we are all the same,

we still live in the same world

fighting to keep sane.

Love As Invasion
by Ryan Buynak

before the sun,

when the world

is still dark

from the past,

I lay awake,

excited to envision

mornings with her

nestled in the crevice

between my neck

and broken shoulder.

it is here,

in this alien invasion

where I want

to live, long,

from the hollow

month of March

to the next mile.

from under doors,

in through windows,

the cracks of broken hearts,

love seeps in like water,

altering everything it touches.

like osmosis alien light,

where the only recourse

is to accept or

burn it down

like an old church

infested with termites.

ALIENATED/AT HOME/ON A SEPARATE PLANET
BY PERNILLE MO

Will I ever find a home better than this space

of time — full of difficult emotions, glimpses

of light and unhappy endings, I blossom.

Unfortunate for my sheer skin, I am

comfortable in this space. Will I ever be more

myself than inside this apartment, inside this

feeling of alienation, like what is outside these

four walls doesn't exist.

Misunderstood by anyone uncomfortable, this

is it. May I shed layers not spacious enough

for these two hours Monday morning where I

have never been so lonely,

and never so happy.

COMMISERATE AND CAPTURE
BY EZRA NOLAN

Empty, and shaking again. Every morning, I hover about this ugly place
I call my home going from bottle to bottle, ever desperate for a bottle
that isn't empty, and shaking. Every morning, I curse myself. Wretch I
am, I can never bring myself to leave the tiniest bit of booze for myself
in the future, even though I know that empty, and shaking bottles are
certainly what the future holds. I find myself again hungry for heaven,
hell, or hooch when divine providence comes to my aid. I've come to
find God has some truly funny ways of loving me. I cursed my clumsy
nature last night as I spilled my drink, but I realized that this was just
God's gift for me. God knows me so well! With shaking hands, I ring
the rag dry and consume it's caustic cocktail. Above disgust, I feel the
burning relief of a day that's bound to be fruitful. So begins my quest to
find enough money around my place to buy booze. Having money
always helps with this sickness, but alas all of my money goes into this
sickness. This is why it's good to have a friend, which I do!
Unfortunately, my friend is a wastrel as well. Putting my clothes on
correctly is becoming more and more of a struggle every day, but
against the odds, I make it happen, and I'm ready to begin the hunt. I
open the door of my trailer and am greeted with the stale slice of Earth

called Roswell, New Mexico. God bless me, and give me luck on this hunt of mine.

One full binge later, I find myself with less clothes on my body than I left my house with. I find it's just as easy for me to lose my clothes as it is difficult to get them on. We all have special skills and talents that God blesses us with. While keeping my clothes on isn't a gift I possess, keeping what little wits I have about me when waking up in strange, new places is one of them. Tonight, it happens to be in the middle of the desert. It's nice to be shaking from the cold, and not alcohol withdrawal. As strange as it sounds, I much prefer waking up like this than at my house. There are a couple of different reasons for this: for one thing, I love a good adventure. Another reason is that I somehow or another always manage to wake up with booze on me in situations like this. The evening air is brisk as it kisses every inch of bare flesh my habits found fit to offer. The liquor however, is a fire that sparks every red cell in my veins back into motion, and again the night is ready to be set ablaze. I wonder what became of my compatriot in chaos. Billy is his name. He's my buddy, my amigo. I spend time with him most nights, and most nights tend to get blurry before one, or both of us black out. Here starts that good, good adventure that I love so much. I start my search in the most rational way I can think to. I swig my bottle, and scream his name loudly into the big, dead mouth that is the New Mexico desert. After some time of screaming for a purpose, I give up on finding my friend and begin to just scream for fun. I like screaming into the desert, it's always been quite cathartic for me. Life and living have always been confusing for me. I've never felt like I belong on this planet. Aside from my buddy, and my amigo, people scare me, and I don't know how to be around them. The desert is peaceful for me, I never feel scared here. Solidarity is security for me, because I know exactly how I can hurt me, anything else is welcoming a spectrum of pain that I'm too much of a coward to face. My drinking and screaming continues, as I treat the desert like a trash can for all of my feelings. Take my pain, take my lonely, and take all of my fury. Turn my anguish into your breath, you dead, yet screaming mouth. Suddenly from nowhere, the mouth speaks back. A light like I've never seen before. I know it sounds odd to consider a light unfamiliar, but this is completely unlike anything I've seen before. Dim, but seeming to come from every direction, I find myself engulfed by it. The light grows brighter, as does my fear, and my anger. How dare this light invade my security? How dare it impede on my peaceful screaming? How is it making my head hurt? Why is everything going black? Is this how I die?

II

Josiah knows how not to die. It's one of the things that impresses me most about him. He also knows how to keep to himself,

113

and that's something I like too. I can't ever seem to do that. I like being around other people even though people don't seem to like me back. I like spending time with him, but I don't rightly mind when he wanders off to where ever it is he goes. It gives me the chance to pretend like I'm charming at one of the local bars. There's an interesting mix of drunkards in Roswell, and the surrounding area. We've got people who was and is in the military, washed up scientists left over from Dr. Goddard's rocket experiments, guys who were German prisoners of war from World War Two, and a bunch of their weird kids. Life's always been sad, and hopeless for me. For some reason watching these people come together after all they've been forced to go through makes me feel a little bit better, though. Josie likes screaming into the desert, I like talking with these people. Tonight's conversations are lively, and interesting. The one I'm having is with one of those washed up scientists. He spends most of his time here trying to talk about science with anyone who isn't a scientist. We're talking about this thing called "The Fermi Paradox". I've never heard of it before, but this Fermi guy reckons that with all the stars in the sky, there's probably got to be aliens out there, or something. I don't know enough about the subject to really talk back to the man, and I think he likes it that way. Josie is the smart one of us, I'm the nice one. I think that's one thing that troubles him, now that I think about it. Maybe I wouldn't like this man as much if I was smart enough to know what he's talking about. I like to listen,

114

though. It makes me feel like I'm connecting with other people. Josie talks about how he feels like an alien a lot of the times. I wonder which one of those stars he thinks he comes from? I wonder if he'd feel more comfortable if he made his way back home? I wonder how he would get there. I asked the scientist about that when I got a chance to speak. He knows Josie, and reckons he's a crazy religious zealot, and told me that I shouldn't worry about anything he thinks. He said that it's mathematically impossible for aliens to visit us even if they do exist. If aliens can't exist, what does that mean for Josie and me? Are we really just bad at being people? Is the hope that we're born of something more than human just a crazy dream we have to lessen our discomfort? I don't think I'll ever know, but I'm glad Josiah hates people too much to ever have this conversation with this man. I don't think he can handle it. I wonder where he is now?

III

Hot, my body is hot, and I'm wet. I haven't even opened my eyes yet, and I'm already uncomfortable with the fresh new hell this day has to offer. Against my better judgment, I decide to continue to live as I open my eyes to a blinding light. It's a familiar light, though. I know this light. It's my warm, loving sun. I'm in the desert again, it's morning, and I'm wet from sweat as the desert heat begins to turn itself into the unforgiving oven it becomes during every day. What became of me last night? What havoc did I rage against my body? I remember falling asleep angry. I remember living afraid, and confused before falling asleep angry. Anything else aside from that is alcohol vapor distilling behind my eyes, and condensing along the inside of my mind to slowly drip back into a blurred memory. As I try to piece together my final moments of consciousness from the night before, something strikes me. I don't mean that I was struck physically, but the blow was just as swift. I can't feel myself shaking. It's morning, and my hands are steady. Am I still drunk from last night? I do find myself feeling a little too happy for the morning. That's it, by the grace of God, I'm still drunk as I begin this morning's quest! I spare no time in making my way to Billy's house this morning, lest I waste this morning's blessing. Billy isn't the recluse I am. Billy loves people, and being around them. He's my counterpart in this way. He lives deep in the heart of town, and I loathe it with every pulse on most of my morning walks. On this mysteriously blessed day, I find the buildings gleaming, and spectacular. The roads are sparkling, and clean. I don't even mind the sound of people gleefully chattering to each other as I pass along the sidewalk. Things are different today, and I'm not even in a panic about it. I'm not even in a panic about how at ease I feel about everything. For the first time, maybe in my life, I feel at home as I walk to Billy's home. "What do I do with all of this comfort?!" I scream to the town people. Seemingly from nowhere, I hear a voice say "feelin' good today, Josiah?" It was Billy, but honestly, I was almost ready for it to be anybody else. Again, no panic. "Yes Bill,

I'm feeling quite more alive than I believe I've ever felt, and I don't know how to handle it at the moment." As I said those words, I realized that this was in fact true. I was ready for anything the day had to come. Darkness, depravity, and death exist not on this day. Last night I died, but my life didn't end. I feel like today is the first day of eternity!

IV

A good mood? I've never seen Josiah this happy in the morning before. He's usually a shaking catastrophe who can't handle a handshake, let alone happiness. I can understand how it would be confusing to him, but it somehow or another isn't sending him into a crazy rage fit like confusion usually does. It's also strange to see him on a main street this deep into town. He usually knows better than to show is face around town for too long. In addition to being one of my best friends, he's also the people's pariah. Nobody really gets him, and he doesn't mind it that way. That's why we're different, and that's what I envy about him. The part of that I don't envy is when it gets him into trouble. People don't get that he sees things his own way, and he sometimes gets angry when the world doesn't see things like he does. I understand why he's like that. It's hard for him to be kind when he's hurt. At least that's what he says. Around once a month someone catches him going to the store, and he catches a punch to the face. He does seem different today. He seems like he's unpunchable or something. I put all of that aside, and figure he'll want to get down to business. Beer is how we usually start our day. We're not animals, we save grain alcohol for the evening. Beer is for all the time. I ask him if he's ready to make a trip to the store for some beer. I'll never forget the first time he said no to a beer. My surprise must have shown on my face because right away he said "I don't know what it is about today, but I feel like I don't need a beer right now. Maybe later, friend. The day is still alive."

V

Watching the sunset beyond the mountains is one of the few pleasures I have left. It's the only reason I stuck around this place after the war. The people here make it difficult to want to hang around though. Not all of them, actually most are nice, I really mean two people in particular. Josiah and his damned friend Billy. Josiah is my neighbor, and Billy is his idiot sidekick. Never have I seen a tighter pair of bugger mates. I don't rightly know if they're queers, but they damn sure spend enough time with each other to raise some questions with me. Always drunk, always starting trouble. I'm glad they're nowhere to be seen as I watch the world's gift to me. This moment is a happy place for me, and I treasure the wits I have about me so's I can maintain all of it. Unlike that good for nothing bag of dirt who lives next door to me. It's been too many years I've had to hear him screaming about God, and life, and death. He keeps it on, I'll show him his death. Killing a man would be nothing to me. I served a tour in the Pacific, and Europe during the WW2 before having to take a damn job at the POW prison here in New

Mexico. The screams I heard during all of that time is almost nothing compared to the screams of this damn lunatic. This Josiah, this Billy. These moaning jackasses have destroyed all the peace I tried to find in living here. I'm not the only one who thinks that, either. I've got plenty of people in town on my side who don't want these fools around no more. I've got some buddies I drink with at the VFW I might go see later tonight. We'll see if he'll be a problem here much longer. I don't remember who it was I heard it from, but I heard some one say the desert is a big dead mouth. I don't rightly know if I know what that means, but if that's true, I'm gonna feed that mouth something soon...

VI

It's sunset, and Josie hasn't had a drink all day. I've even been keeping it lighter because I want to help him out. We're trying to put together his night last night, and why he's feeling so good today. I usually have a hard time understanding him when he gets all philosophical or whatever he calls it, but today it extra weird. If talking to the science man last night had me a little confused, talking to Jo had me outright baffled. After a little while of silence and sunset he asks me "Bill, do you ever think about all of the colors you'll never see? Do you ever look up into the stars and wonder if the eyes that look back do the same math as we do? What's on the other side of life, Bill?" "Josie, I've never thought about any of that in my life. I talked to a fella last night what reckons there ain't possibly no aliens, and if there is, there ain't no

119

way they can make it here." Just like I thought, Josiah didn't look to happy to hear that. "Another man's nihilism shouldn't hinder our potential for higher thought, William." He never calls me William, nobody ever calls me that. What happened to him last night? I barely know what happened to myself last night. I do remember what bar it all happened at though. "Do you want to go talk to that science guy I met last night? He might be at the same bar again. I don't remember much of last night, but I remember what bar I was at." I asked him that even though I know he hates going to bars. He hates drinking around too many people because of all the trouble it gets him into. "That's a brilliant idea, Bill. You're a gift from the almighty!" He said yes? Josiah is going to go back into a bar? This has been a day full of surprises, and I don't know what to make of any of them. I doubt this'll be the last surprise of my night.

VII

My dad and I never really had too much in common outside of our military uniforms, our hatred of my mother, and a love of bars. Sometimes I wonder if I would be happier if I made the same dumb mistake as that old man. Sitting around at the VFW bar wipes that all away. I remember that my family is right here, and here is a great place to be. I get to spend most nights the way that I really want to spend them. Silent, and in the company of bubbly drinks instead of bubbly women. Now don't get me wrong, I ain't no queer or nothin'. I just can't

120

deal with all the dang jibber-jabber, so I don't. There aren't any women in this here bar, only other fellas. Not too many other fellas, either. The ones that are here, I quite enjoy having around. They don't like talking, and we have that in common. Now that I think about it, I'd go so far as to say that I have more in common with all of these men than I have with my old man. These fellas here are the kind of drunks I've always wanted to be, but my old man is the drunk I became. Maybe that's why I don't like myself very much. I've got a lot of that dirty old dog in me, and I don't like it. I even find myself smelling like he did as a scratch myself alone in my chair. I can even feel myself growing angry and dumb just like he did, and I didn't even need a family to do it. How's that for generational advancement? All of that doesn't seem to matter here. Maybe that's why we all chum around like we do? We all know that outside of these here walls, none of us are worth a nickel compared to most of these ungrateful idiots who never fought for anything. Here I am, a man who defended the rights, and freedoms of his countrymen. A man who fought to keep people from living like that damn heathen hitler wanted us to live! I fought to keep people livin' happy, healthy, and free. Now, I don't got no pot to piss in. When I was a kid, I thought everybody deserved to live as they please, and nobody needed nobody tellin' them what to do or who to do it with. Now, I just think I hated that old dog of a dad tellin' me what to do. I'll tell you what, nothing really crushes a man quite like realizing that maybe hitler wasn't all that wrong. I mean, I ain't got nothin' against nobody like he had, and I never thought like that for most of my life. I don't even hate nobody to the point of killing all of them off, but I get what he means by undesirables. God damn Josiah, and Billy those pieces of dung. Watching those fools live the way they live is like watching someone piss on a rose garden you did your best to tend to and love for years and years. Actually, they did do that to me. I used to love my rose garden until it betrayed me by smelling of their piss. Yeah, that was a few years ago, but I'll never forgive them for as long as any of us live. When you fight for someone's freedom, you forget that means they're free to piss you off, and live next door to you. I don't know if I hate freedom, or if I hate them, or if I just hate their freedom, but I know I hate thinking about it. I don't reckon I know what the word is, but I really hate that these two make me understand what hitler was on about. Maybe some people are inferior, and if there are undesirable people, Josiah and Bill are two of them. Sometimes me and the boys around the bar talk about how many of our problems we could solve if they just wasn't around. They don't live next door to them idiots, so they ain't got as much to say about the matter as I do, but we all agree that the whole planet would be better off without them two. I never told them that thing about hitler though. Oh, what I wouldn't give to be alone in a locked room with them, a bunch of weapons, and no consequences. Funny that they're free to wave their ass while I wave my flag, but I'm not free to bury those asses. I was trained to buy people to protect MY freedom. Now they expect me to just sit around while these damn fools just make my country worse? I fought for my freedom, not them. What right do they have to act like this? What right do they have to freedom? Who the hell can tell me that I'm wrong because I use the training I was given to protect my country from these damn wackadoos? I hope that fool's god is listening, because he'd better help me if I catch that boy tonight!

5+3a

"Be diligent in your observation" the one said to the other. "Mathematics dictates that our encounter is soon to occur. Be ready to act with haste, and for not a single moment will you let your attention falter."

IX

"I don't see why you thought that experience would upset me, Bill. That scientist was a lovely man!" Now that it's over, I agree with Josiah. I don't know why I thought that experience would upset this particular version of him. I didn't think about how much his good mood would change how he usually acted. As we leave the bar, I thought about how I don't think I've ever seen Josiah in a good mood and sober. "Now that I think about it, I can see why you'd assume that I wouldn't have been too keen on that interaction. You'd usually be right in that assumption, Bill. For a scientist, I found the man rather charming. He's a very knowledgeable man, and I appreciate that. I must say that I found

123

his lack of faith disturbing, but I could say that about almost any man of science." The streetlights are on, as we walk trough town. Engaging, and familiar Jo and I walk down the street towards my house in near silence. I've always really liked walking with my friend at night. There aren't usually very many people out this late, and the ones who are out are usually too drunk, or in their own business to care about a couple of guys like us. Usually we'd never have to talk to anybody but each other. This is why it was strange when some guy out of the dark called out "Hey, Josiah and Billy I got something for you two!" I couldn't make out who it was, but I knew enough to figure he didn't have anything good for us. I yell back "We're okay, buddy. Josie and I are going to just keep to ourselves tonight, we've got a problem we're trying to solve." Almost before I can finish speaking I hear the man shout "YOU TWO QUEERS ARE ABOUT TO HAVE A BIGGER PROBLEM!" The man ran towards us with an intensity that I found kind of unnecessary. Just before he got under the streetlight to where we could have seen him, an even brighter light hit, and blinded us all. The surprises aren't stopping tonight.

T'en(d)

One says to the other: "It's alright, they're safe now. You can shut off the machine." The soft hum that filled the room slowly dies down. I can't see who said those words as my vision is blurry. The way the air is touching me feels different, but familiar. I'm hearing sounds

124

that I know I've heard before but can't seem to place. In spite of all of my senses being either dulled or confused, I remain calm. Almost as if someone is pumping an unyielding supply of assurance into the space behind my eyes. Slowly, my senses and more come back to me. As I regain my vision, the storm cloud in my brain begins to dissipate. I remember this place, but I don't remember why. There's something new about the room, though. Billy is here with me this time. I don't know why, but I know he hasn't ever been here before. "Jo, is that you? Where are we?" Before I can answer, I see them again. The two beings I've seen in every dream I've ever forgotten! I now begin to panic for the first time in what feels like a long time. However, that only lasts for a moment. I don't know how, but I can feel these beings speaking feelings into my mind. Again, I'm calm. Calm in spite of the fact that I'm beginning to realize the entire life I lived was a lie. I've spent a lot of time wondering what role God plays in our lives as humans on Earth. Was I wrong to think that, or was I actually on the right path? Is it so far past the realm of believable that these things dictate everything that happens on earth? An orchestra conductor dictates an entire symphony while not making a sound himself, after all. Are these beings the god I thought I knew this whole time? I realized that nothing is binding me to the table. I sit up, and ask them who they are, and why they brought Billy and me here, and where in fact "here" is. In unison they answer: We're your family, you two are our brothers. Welcome home!

125

El Extraterrestre
By Enid Nolasco

Alien: not belonging

Uninvited, like that (really good) Alanis song

Other

Foreign

Alien: a really good movie

I cringe at the term illegal alien

There isn't a word for alien in Spanish

There is for extraterrestrial

For other-worldly

Alien is as foreign to the Spanish language as

We all are to this land

Yes, there are laws

Laws of nature

Laws of physics (at least for now)

Laws of the people

The concept of an action being illegal

Understandable

The concept of a person being illegal

Now, that is alien.

QUARK WAS RIGHT
BY SARAH ELGATIAN

Mack,

I'm sorry. I really am. It's my fault you were brought into this mess and
I understand if you won't forgive me.

See, we were never meant to meet. I want to call it fate--our chance
encounter at the supermarket three times in a row--but Corona is such a
small town and you were just some guy.

You were supposed to be some guy.

See, you didn't know that I wasn't a nice girl from out-of-town and I
assumed that you weren't very bright. I suppose we were both kind of
right.

You walked me to my car that third time, your green eyes heavily
lidded, a little bit of sweat gathering at your temples. You said you were
going to buy a refrigerator. I pretended to be impressed. You asked me
out to pie across the street. I stuttered, which you must have thought was

nerves rather than shock. I accepted feeling like a pioneer, a pilgrim. Was this success in the promised land?

You were the first person outside of my colleagues that I spent any time with. I assumed this made me successful but you were more observant than I expected and I was more poorly camouflaged than I thought. Ffffffffffffffff ffffff ffffffff fffffff fff ffffffff words words word. Words. Words words words words words. Words words. The hubris, I know.

Still, our brains fill in the blank spaces and question marks and I got from you the one thing I believed meant that we fit in: you were attracted to me. Your pupils dilated, your heartbeat increased, you couldn't take your eyes off of me. I ought to have been nervous, but honestly, what a thrill.

When I reported back to my colleagues about my trip to the grocer, the reviews were mixed. Rom was ecstatic, Quark suspicious. Redact redact redact redact redact redact words words. Words.

Quark was right. Because you were *such* a man. What kind of charm did you think I would see when you followed me home? Is this what women in New Mexico like? Women in America? Nog had bet me that being a woman would be a disaster, said I didn't have the guts to take this form. Redacted words redacted words. I didn't know that gender was so complicated here, but, really, who cares? I won the bet.

Anyway, this is your Dear John letter. With this I assume you will understand that you have created a goddamn incident and your interest in women is alarming. Redacted words, redacted. I enjoyed your company, I appreciate that you took pride in the rough callouses around your hands and how hard you tried to keep your hair parted evenly to impress me.

But you fell, we tripped, into each other's arms by accident and in denial until we couldn't any longer deny that it was my arms keeping your skin from tearing and your arms keeping my skeleton in tact. And that is not a love story. It is also not safe.

See, you were my catalyst. For change, for creation, for action, for loving.

But now you're my prison. And it isn't your fault that I'm stuck but it's you keeping me here. I wonder if you knew to be afraid of my growth and so your love quit pushing me to grow and started pulling me toward you.

That was a huge mistake. Because I am not like you and all the urgency you assumed? It was my first experience with interpersonal relationships and if you had ever seen without this dress, with my redact Fffffffffffffff ffffff ffffffff f fffffff fff fffffffff words wo rds word. Words. Words wo rds words words words. Words

words. Fffffffffffffff ffffff ffffffff ffffffff fff fffffffff words words word. Words. Words words words words words. Words

words. Fffffffffffffff ffffff ffffffff ffffffff fff fffffffff words words word. Words. Words words words words words. Words

words. Fffffffffffffff ffffff ffffffff ffffffff fff fffffffff words words word. Words. Words words words words words. Words

words. Fffffffffffffff ffffff ffffffff ffffffff fff fffffffff words words word. Words. Words words words words words. Words words.

You get it, right?

The point is: you deserve this. The scrutiny and disbelieving and forever having to explain that you're not crazy. It's my fault and I'm sorry. But you made your bed and if you expect anyone to believe that any of this

is because of extra-terrestrial life came to this planet, to Corona, New

Mexico, to where you happened to be, no proof of that you

were *innocently* following a young woman who was relatively new to

town, well, then you deserve this mess.

All I have left in my heart--learning who you are, learning how much

damage I could have, no *we* could have caused-- is two empty hands a

list of the million ways you proved you weren't the one for me.

I want to leave you with all the love you deserve, all the love that no one

gave you, but I know that you won't take it. I know that you won't

believe me.

But I've got it here for you. It's tied with twine and packaged tightly. I

kept my tentacles and oil from damaging it. I know it won't mean a

damn thing because you need to be your own hero, but it's dangerous to

go alone, take this.

Aliens? You fool.

Goodbye,

Ishka

ROSWELL 1947
BY KENDRA RALSTON

how are you?

i ask her,

making up my mind to not drown everyday

she tells me,

as though we can wade through uncertainty

and tread through the abyss

one sweltering summer to the next

baked in heat and dust and air

basking in our own oven

of helplessness and despair —

not knowing

we'd be gutted by debris

casualties of love and war

and awake

in the infinite

CRASH LANDING
BY ERIN POLTENOVAGE

Sometimes things are not what they seem —

    or maybe they are just not what we want them to be.

We want the world to sparkle just a little bit more –

    or at all,

    so we can feel like we matter.

And so, we see what we want to see.

We see magic in the mundane.

    We credit religion instead of luck,

        or science,

    Conspiracy theories in spite of facts,

    'Premonitions', not mental illness.

    We see aliens instead of government fuckups.

We put faith in the fantastical because life can be so damn boring

    without the make-believe we invent to make it all seem worth

    it.

We want to be the only witness,

      the first to discover some new truth.

      We want so badly to be important that we rarely see what's

      right in front of

us.

Yea,

      there was a crash,

      but no flying discs or green antennas -

      just a pile of foil and desperations begging to be heard.

CRATER
BY ICON303

I watched a comet crash,

I watched a comet crash

And the lights all came.

Sirens and flashes,

Broomsticks and badges,

And they all want to know

If I saw anything strange.

I watched a comet crash,

I watched a comet crash

In faces I've never seen.

Beards and mustaches,

Suits and sunglasses,

And they want me to know

Weathers been acting strange.

I watched a comet crash,

Exploding into balderdash

And driving the locals insane.

Its wasn't a secret military stash

Or held-up escaping gas,

I watched a comet crash...

Simple and plain.

ALIEN IN THE MIRROR
BY TIA MORRISON

Mirrors reflect ones true self. And yet when I gaze into the mirror it seems as if it's a portal to another soul. This person staring back at me carries hollow eyes. Blurred vision in focus to the galaxies of trauma. A past that has landed beyond where Lucifer had fallen. Where you lay in darkness. In nothing. Empty. This person in the mirror is still breathing, still living but not alive. An alien. Because no human can sustain the pressure of zero gravity. Of nothingness. For suffocating in space is the same as drowning in the ocean. So surely this is an alien in the mirror. A human with such pull on their core would have surely seen heaven yet they are still fighting through to hell from the emptiness they had plunder into. This mirror is reflecting delusive flaws. And yet it wasn't me but an alien piercing into my foggy star lit eyes.

HEART TRANSPLANT
BY LAUREN CUSSELL

Alien dweeb

Barely heard

But always seen

How in the hell

Do you love someone like me?

You asked me late at night

Softly and sweetly

"Hey so like

Are you some kind of hippie?"

I guess my answer would be

A hippie of sorts

I don't wear a bra

Half of the time

And I don't care what anyone thinks

More than half of the time

Except for you

I think about you

All of the time

And I wanna know

what you're thinking

All of the time

I am a sun beam

Intergalactically speaking

I am a comet

That crash landed

24 years ago

And that's still not enough

I'm still figuring it all out

I'm sensitive

And I have a brain

And if we are all

Only robots

Then beam me back up

To where true love

still exists

ABOUT PARADISIAC PUBLISHING

Paradisiac Publishing is an independent boutique press located in San Diego, CA specializing in comedic and artistic titles. Our parallel imprint (not bound by physical location) Coyote Blood, represents a number of poets, musicians and other artists, nationwide. All of our titles are found on Amazon, at Barnes & Noble as well as many other bookstores of all shapes and sizes, worldwide. Paradisiac Publishing is located inside the Super Secret Bookstore, whose location remains a mystery. Both publishers are regular featured columnists with The Fusion Press.

Learn more at https://www.paradisiacpublishing.com.

www.ingramcontent.com/pod-product-compliance
Lightning Source LLC
Chambersburg PA
CBHW072028170626
46811CB00008B/2993